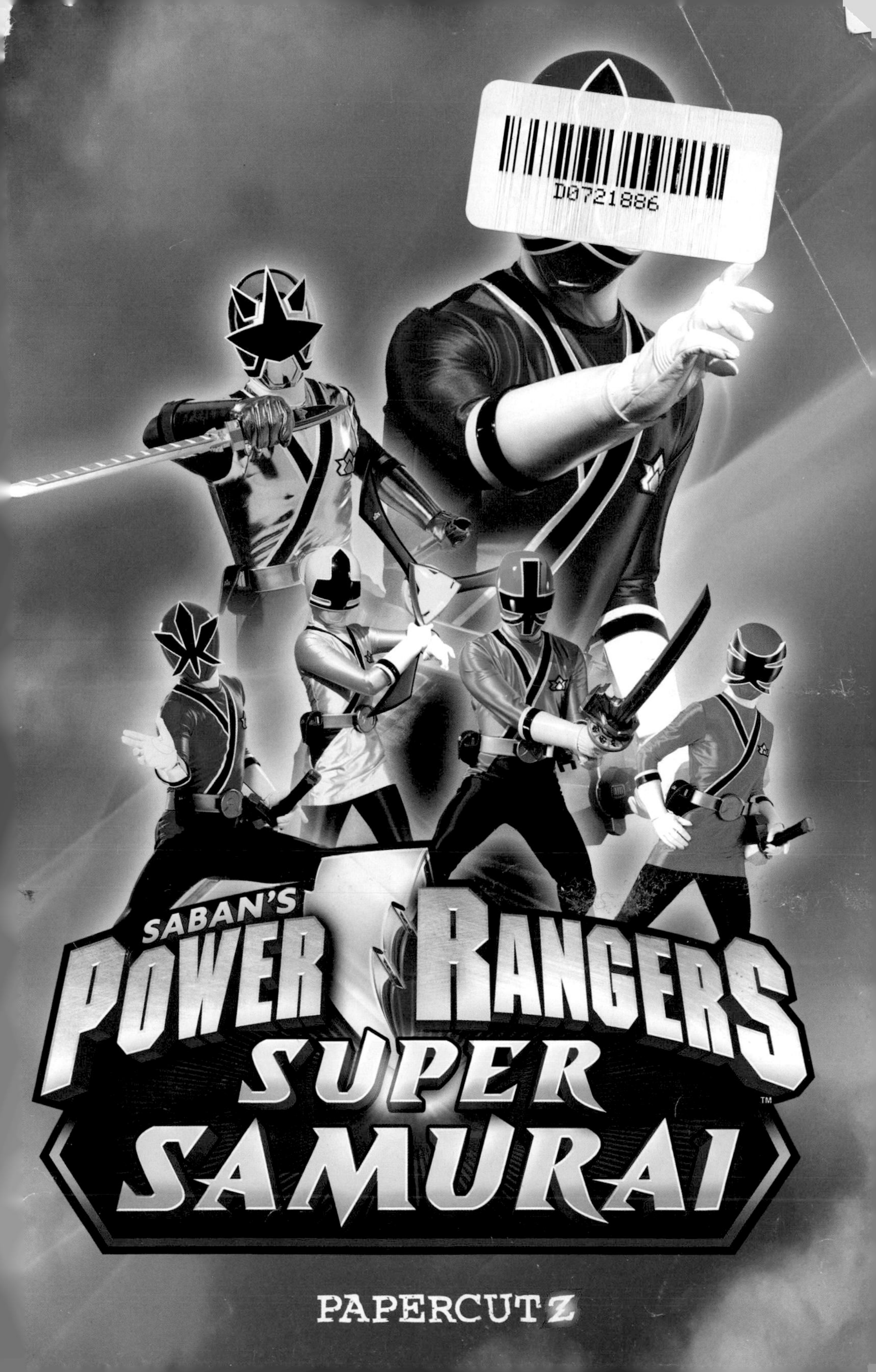
SABAN'S
POWER RANGERS
SUPER SAMURAI
™
PAPERCUTZ

SABAN'S POWER RANGERS SUPER SAMURAI

Graphic Novels Available From PAPERCUTZ

1 "MEMORY SHORT"
SABAN'S POWER RANGERS SUPER SAMURAI
Stefan Petrucha
Paulo Henrique
PAPERCUTZ

Graphic Novel #1

ALL-NEW! GRAPHIC NOVEL
SABAN'S POWER RANGERS SUPER SAMURAI
2 "TERRIBLE TOYS"
Petrucha • Henrique
PAPERCUTZ

COMING SOON: Graphic Novel #2

SABAN'S POWER RANGERS graphic novels are available in paperback and hardcover at booksellers everywhere.

Or order from us: please add $4.00 for postage and handling for first book, add $1.00 for each additional book.
POWER RANGERS graphic novels are $6.99 in paperback, and $10.99 in hardcover. Please make check payable to NBM Publishing.
Send to: Papercutz 160 Broadway, Ste. 700, East Wing, New York, NY 10038 • 1-800-886-1223

www.papercutz.com

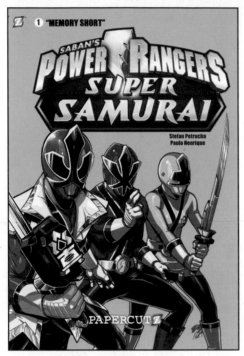

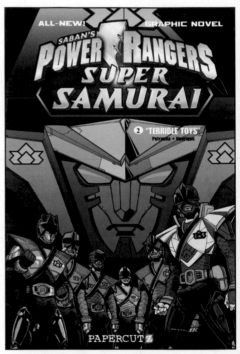

① "MEMORY SHORT"

Stefan Petrucha – Writer

Paulo Henrique – Artist

Laurie E. Smith – Colorist

New York

SABAN'S POWER RANGERS SUPER SAMURAI
#1 "MEMORY SHORT"

STEFAN PETRUCHA – Writer
PAULO HENRIQUE – Artist
LAURIE E. SMITH – Colorist
BRYAN SENKA – Letterer

Production by NELSON DESIGN GROUP, LLC
Associate Editor – MICHAEL PETRANEK
JIM SALICRUP
Editor-in-Chief

ISBN: 978-1-59707-331-8 paperback edition
ISBN: 978-1-59707-332-5 hardcover edition

Printed in Canada
May 2012 by Friesens Printing
1 Printers Way
Altona, MB R0G 0B0

Distributed by Macmillan

First Printing

MEET SABAN'S POWER RANGERS SUPER SAMURAI

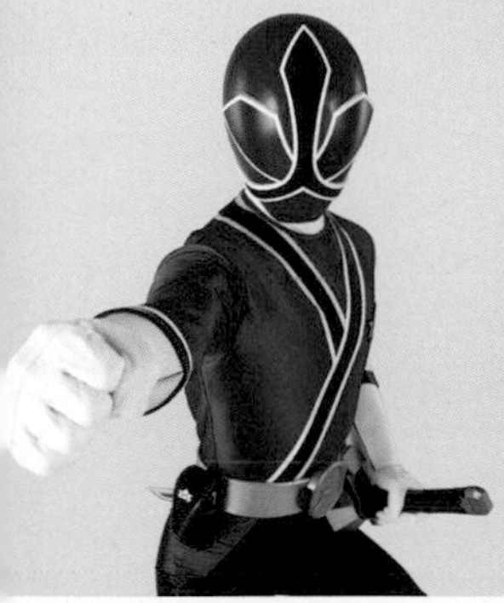

For as long as the Nighlok have existed, there have been Power Rangers sworn to fight them.

The current team of Samurai Power Rangers is a group of teens who grew up knowing that one day they would be summoned to use their uniquely inherited powers and extraordinary skills against evil as the Power Rangers. These skills and powers have been passed down through generation to generation and determine which Ranger they will become.

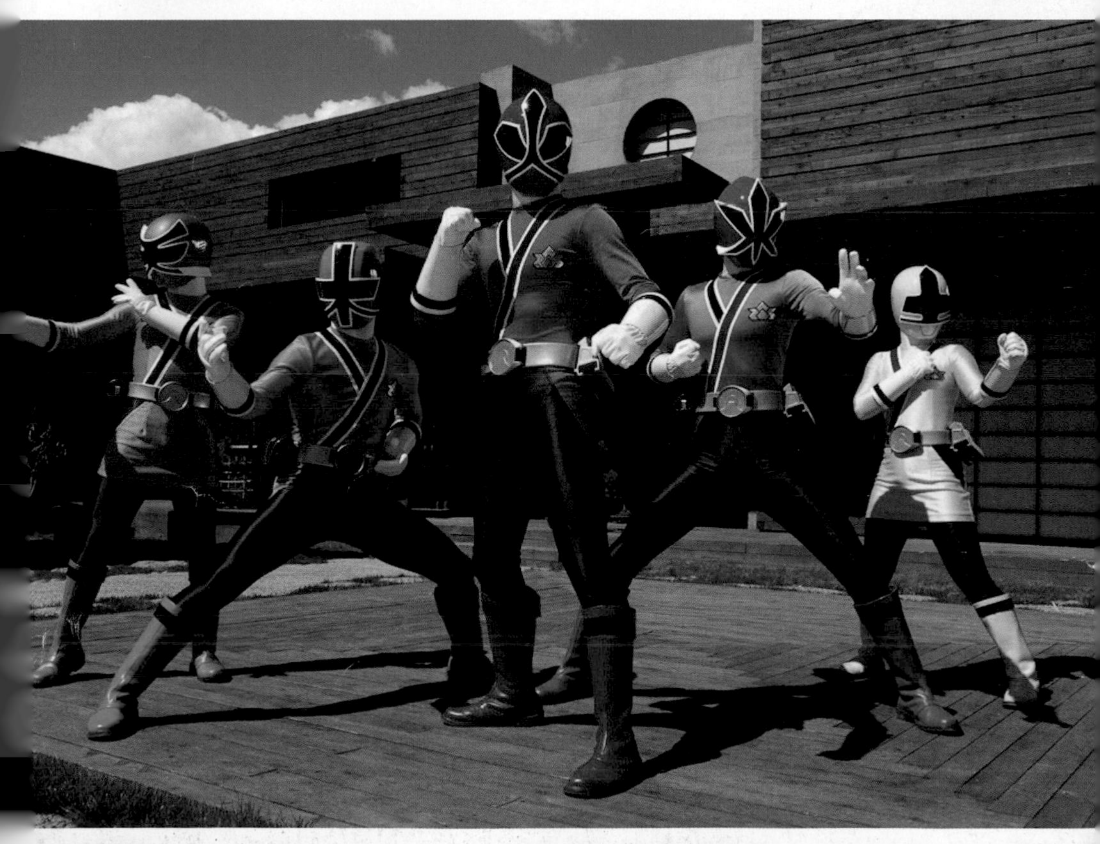

SABAN'S POWER RANGERS SUPER SAMURAI

THE RED RANGER (JAYDEN)

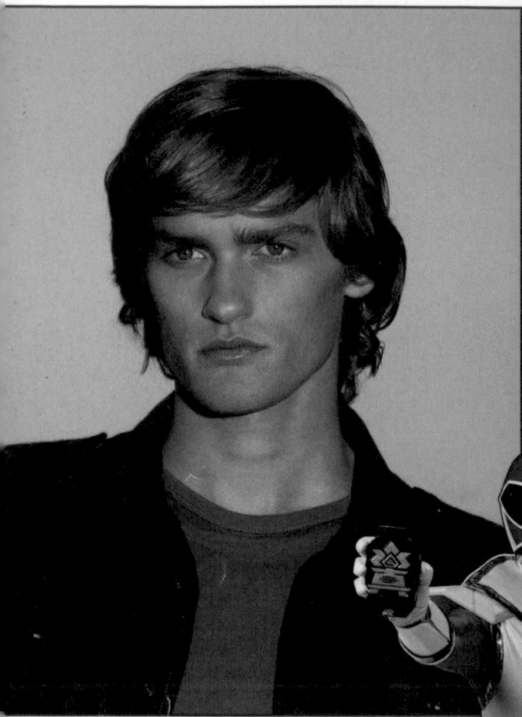

Jayden, the Red Ranger, is the leader of the Samurai Power Rangers. He is a man of few words, but when he speaks he means what he says. He was raised by Mentor Ji after his father died, who was the Red Ranger before him. Jayden has become an excellent warric and has kept the Moogers at bay on his own for some time. Now, with the help of the other Rangers, Jayden is learning to be a leader and what it is like to have true friend.

Jayden is a kind and caring person but can be firm when action calls. He also carries a secret that he cannot reveal t the other Rangers and at times this knowledge causes him conflict.

His element is fire and his Zord is the Lion.

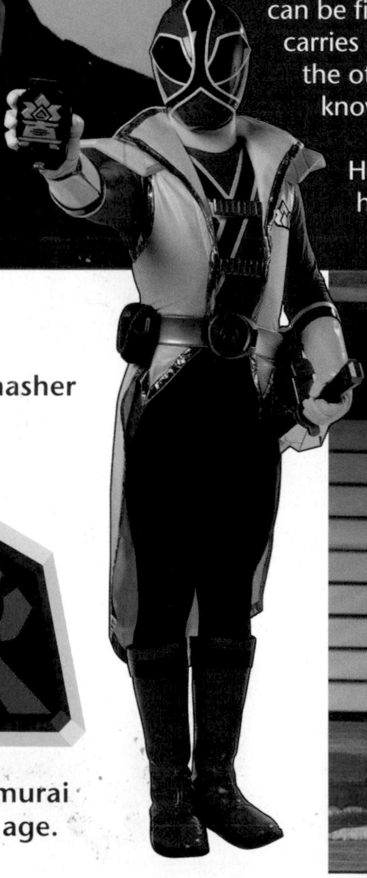

Weapon:
Spin Sword/Fire Smasher

Signature Move:
Fire Smasher!

Element:
Fire

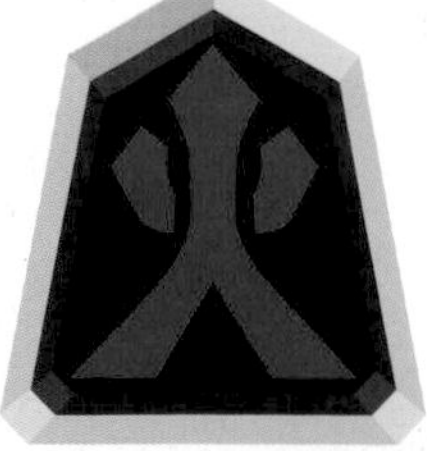

Zord:
Lion

Notes:
Trained to be a Samurai from a very young age.

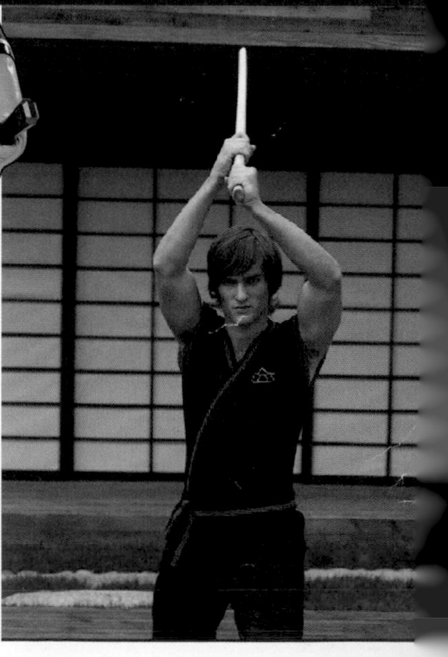

THE PINK RANGER (MIA)

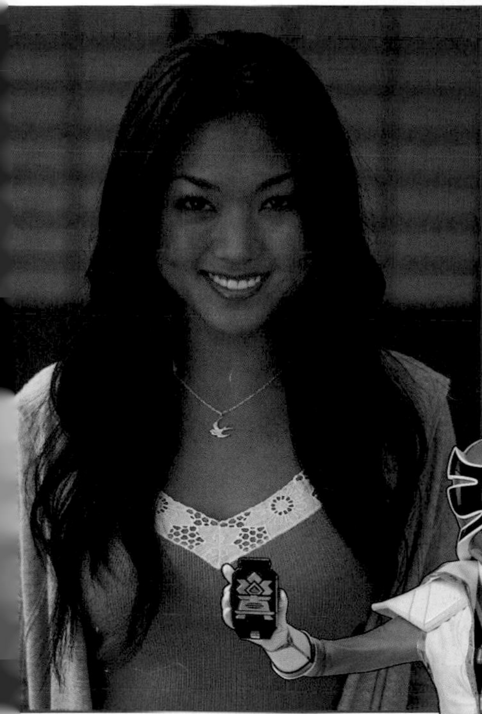

Mia, the Pink Ranger, is the big sister to the group. She is a confident, intuitive, and sensitive person. She is very pragmatic and cares a lot about the well-being of the other Rangers. She trains as hard as the rest of the team, and will jump in to help any Ranger or person in need.

Mia enjoys cooking and often offers up her skills to feed the other Rangers. Problem is that Mia is not a good cook. The humor begins as the other Rangers try their best to act as if her culinary delights are edible.

Mia's element is the sky and her Zord is the Turtle.

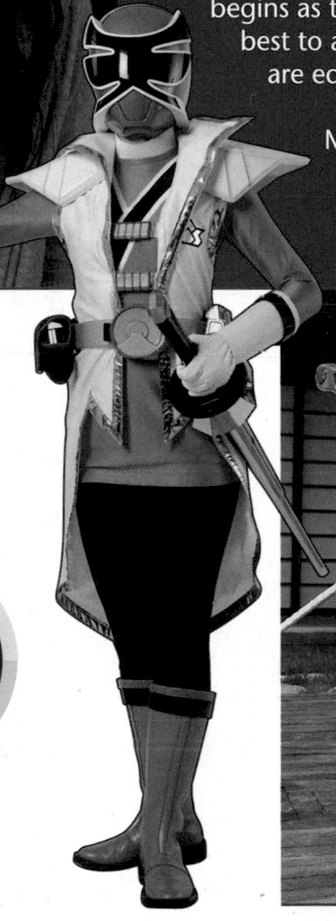

Weapon:
Spin Sword/Sky Fan

Signature Move:
Airway!

Element:
Sky

Zord:
Turtle

Notes:
Longs to be a gourmet chef and used to sing

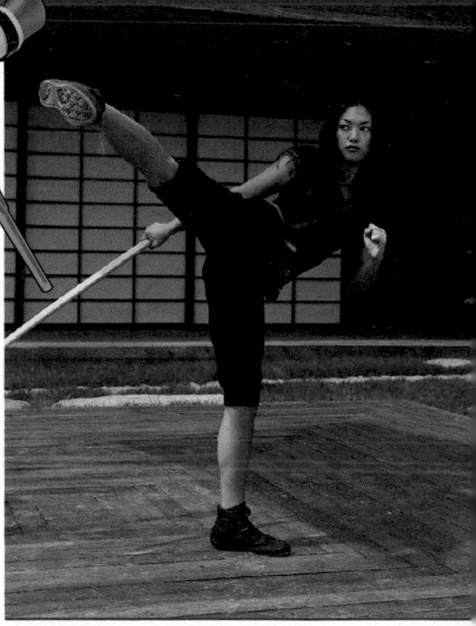

SABAN'S POWER RANGERS SUPER SAMURAI

THE BLUE RANGER (KEVIN)

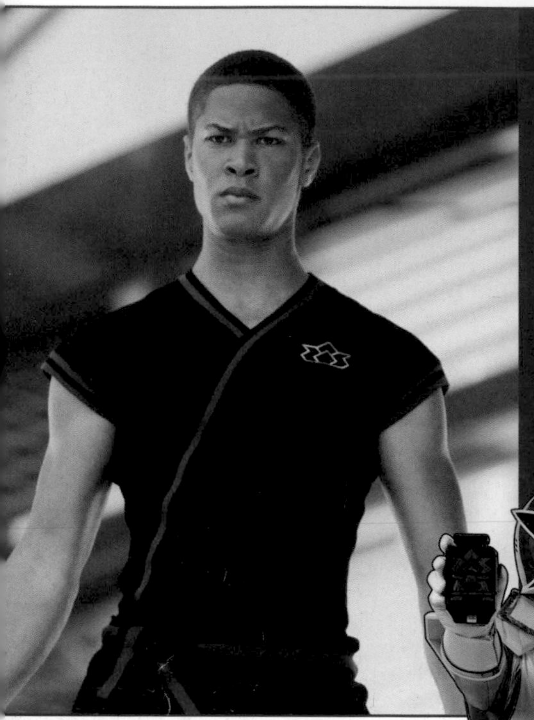

Kevin, the Blue Ranger, has lived his entire life by the code of the Samurai.

Kevin's dream was to be an Olympic swimmer. However, he has placed that dream on hold to become the Blue Ranger. He is a well-trained swordsman and has been raised on the traditions of the Samurai. Kevin is the more sober Ranger who continues his discipline with a daily workout and training. He is honored to be a Samurai and takes his position among the Rangers seriously.

His element is water and his Zord is the Dragon.

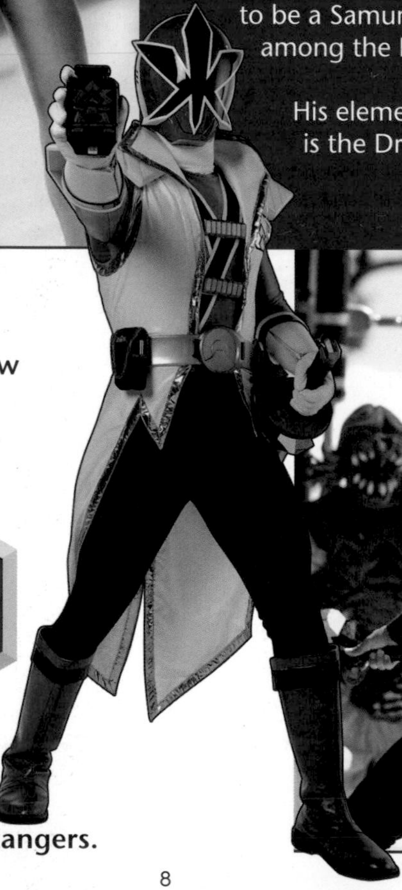

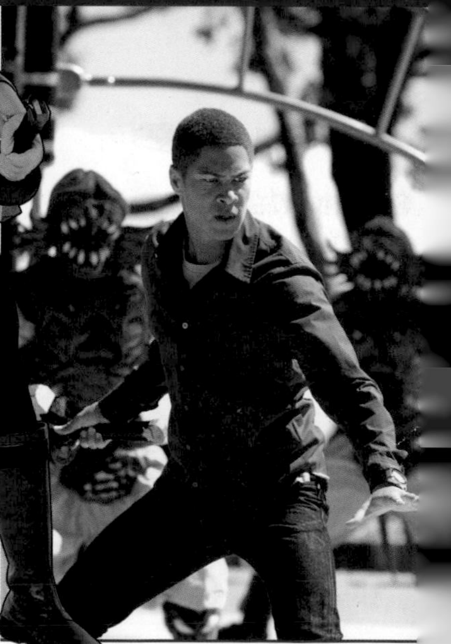

Weapon:
Spin Sword/Hydro Bow

Signature Move:
Dragon Splash!

Element:
Water

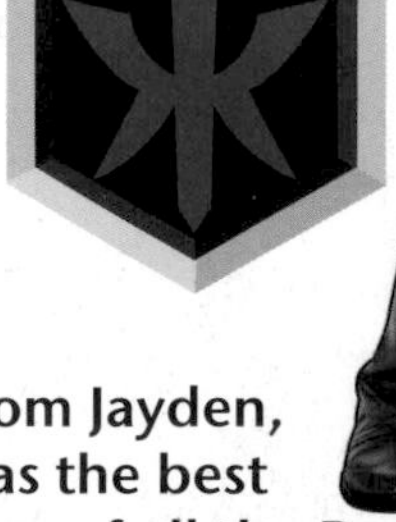

Zord:
Dragon

Notes:
Aside from Jayden, Kevin has the best technique of all the Rangers.

SABAN'S POWER RANGERS SUPER SAMURAI

THE GREEN RANGER (MIKE)

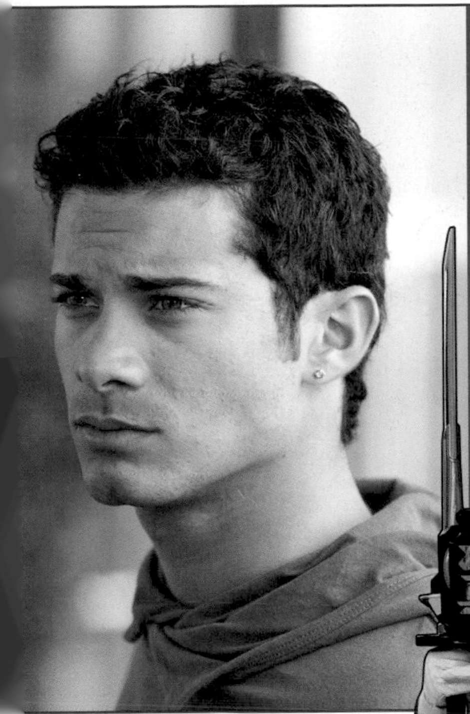

Being a bit of a rebel is truly part of Mike's nature. He is the Green Ranger.

Mike loves to think outside of the box, play video games, and hang with friends. He has a more casual approach to his training but deep down inside takes being a Power Rangers seriously. He is a free spirit and has a great sense of humor. All of his characteristics allow him to come up with new fighting strategies to beat Master Xandred's evil Nighlok. He is a valuable part of the team.

Mike's element is the forest and his Zord is the Bear.

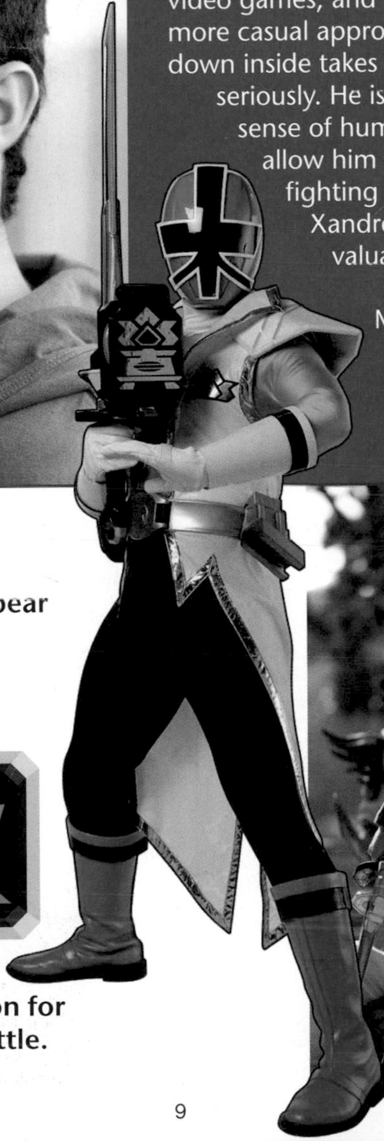

Weapon:
Spin Sword, Forest Spear

Signature Move:
Forest Vortex!

Element:
Forest

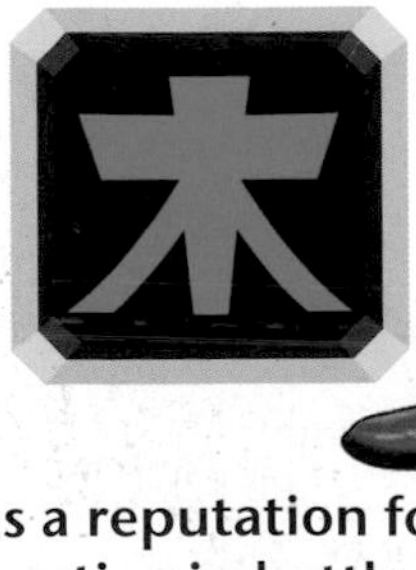

Zord:
Bear

Notes:
Mike has a reputation for being creative in battle.

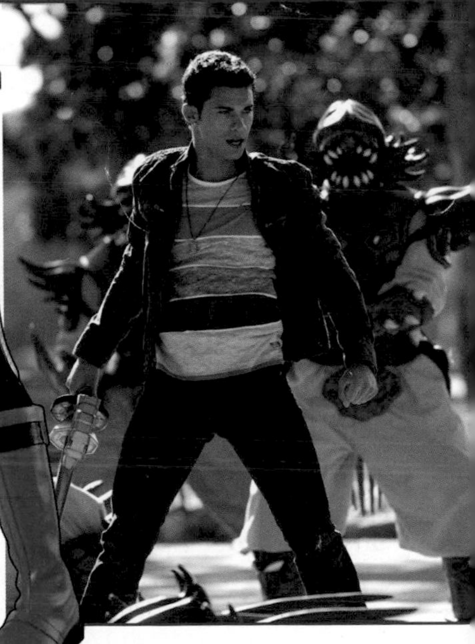

SABAN'S POWER RANGERS SUPER SAMURAI

THE YELLOW RANGER (EMILY)

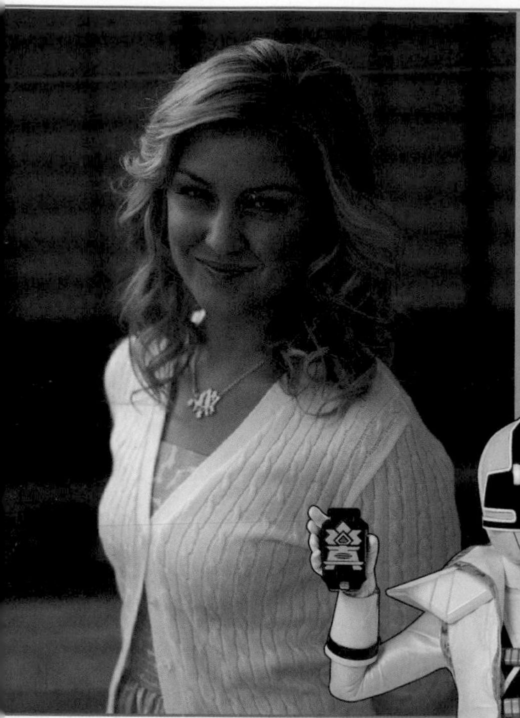

Youngest of the Rangers, Emily is the Yellow Ranger. She is a sweet and kind person who was raised in the country side.

It was actually her sister who was originally to become the Yellow Ranger prior to falling ill. Emily stepped up to the challenge and took her sister's spot on the team. She is determined to make her sister proud and trains harder because of that. She is very musical, and her silliness is infectious. Her wide-eyed optimism often helps the team stay positive when it seems that all the odds are against them.

Emily's element is Earth and her Zord is the Ape.

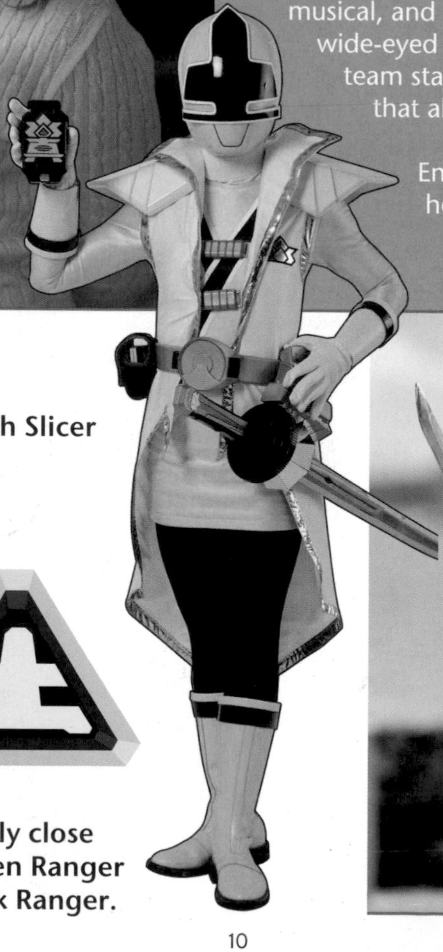

Weapon:
Spin Sword/Earth Slicer

Signature Move:
Seismic Swing!

Element:
Earth

Zord:
Ape

Notes:
Emily is especially close to Mike the Green Ranger and Mia the Pink Ranger.

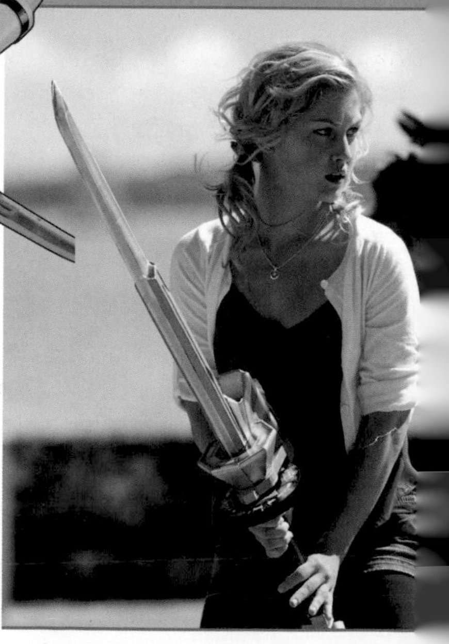

THE GOLD RANGER (ANTONIO)

Antonio is not like the rest of the Power Rangers and is uniquely the Gold Ranger.

Unlike the other five Power Rangers, Antonio did not receive any formal Samurai training and mastered his fighting skills on his own. When he was a young child, he and Jayden were best friends. They practiced the Samurai moves together, but then Antonio's family moved away. Antonio vowed to return and to become a Samurai Power Ranger. Using his computer skills, Antonio was able to create his own Samuraizer, able to program powers and operate his Octozord which was a present from Jayden years before. True to his word, Antonio returns as the Gold Ranger with mastered samurai skills.

His element is light and his Zord is an Octopus known as OctoZord.

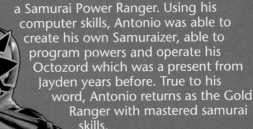

Weapon:
Barracuda Blade

Signature Move:
Barracuda Bite!

Element:
Light

Zord:
Octozord,
Lightzord

Notes:
Antonio is a techie and communicates with his Zord via text messaging.

MASTER XANDRED

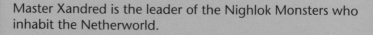

Master Xandred is the leader of the Nighlok Monsters who inhabit the Netherworld.

Jayden's Father, the previous Red Ranger, shattered Master Xandred into a million pieces, vanishing him to the Netherworld forever. Recently Master Xandred awoke and began a reign of terror in an attempt to return to our world. With his trusty advisor, Master Xandred has sent Nighlok to Earth in an attempt to make the humans cry as their tears help raise the Sanzu River. Once the river is high enough, Master Xandred can escape the Netherworld and rule the Earth.

OCTOROO

Octoroo is Master Xandred's trusted advisor. He counsels Master Xandred about the Netherworld and the Nighlok that live there. Often he offers up new plans and tactics to defeat the Rangers. Octoroo is an Octopus-like creature and at times cannot be trusted.

DAYU

Dayu has not always been half human and half Nighlok. She once was a new bride, but she traded her human life centuries ago in an effort to save her husband as a powerful Nighlok promised to spare her husband if she would go with him. The only possession she was allowed to take with her was her guitar which became the "Harmonium." Master Xandred keeps her near because her music soothes him.

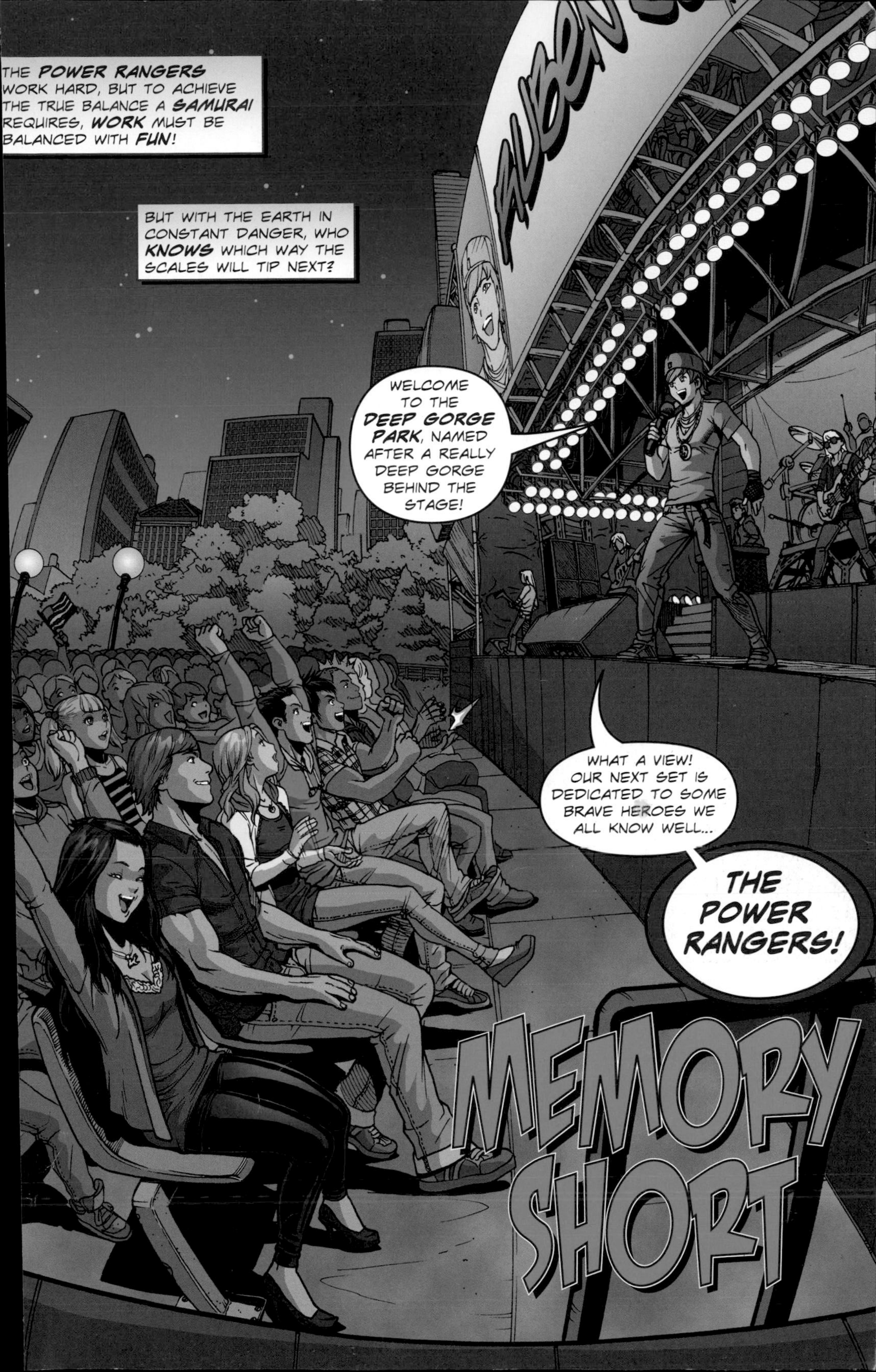
THE POWER RANGERS WORK HARD, BUT TO ACHIEVE THE TRUE BALANCE A SAMURAI REQUIRES, WORK MUST BE BALANCED WITH FUN!
BUT WITH THE EARTH IN CONSTANT DANGER, WHO KNOWS WHICH WAY THE SCALES WILL TIP NEXT?
WELCOME TO THE DEEP GORGE PARK, NAMED AFTER A REALLY DEEP GORGE BEHIND THE STAGE!
WHAT A VIEW! OUR NEXT SET IS DEDICATED TO SOME BRAVE HEROES WE ALL KNOW WELL...
THE POWER RANGERS!
MEMORY SHORT

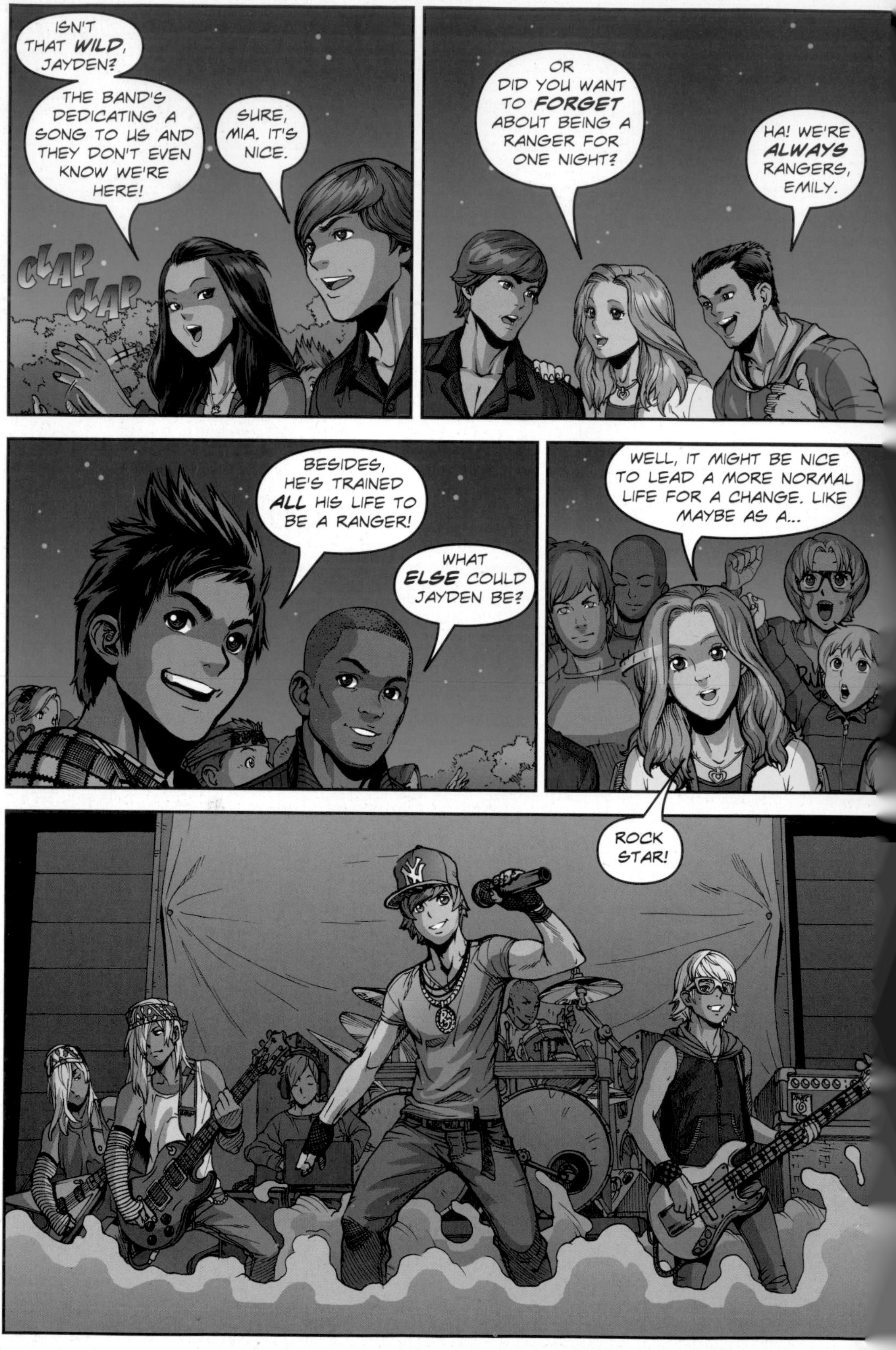
ISN'T THAT WILD, JAYDEN?
THE BAND'S DEDICATING A SONG TO US AND THEY DON'T EVEN KNOW WE'RE HERE!
CLAP CLAP
SURE, MIA. IT'S NICE.
OR DID YOU WANT TO FORGET ABOUT BEING A RANGER FOR ONE NIGHT?
HA! WE'RE ALWAYS RANGERS, EMILY.
BESIDES, HE'S TRAINED ALL HIS LIFE TO BE A RANGER!
WHAT ELSE COULD JAYDEN BE?
WELL, IT MIGHT BE NICE TO LEAD A MORE NORMAL LIFE FOR A CHANGE. LIKE MAYBE AS A...
ROCK STAR!

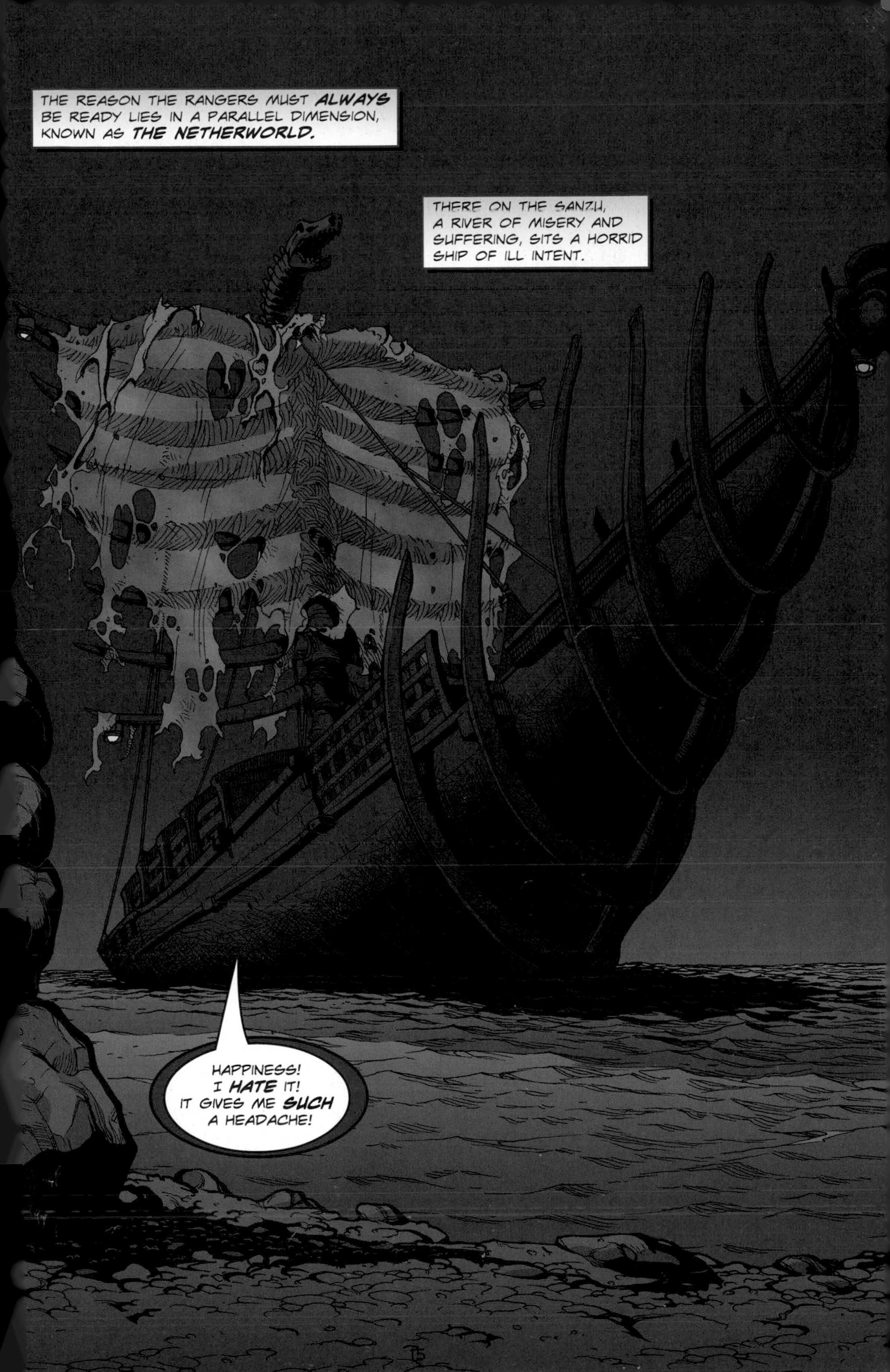
THE REASON THE RANGERS MUST ALWAYS BE READY LIES IN A PARALLEL DIMENSION, KNOWN AS THE NETHERWORLD.
THERE ON THE SANZU, A RIVER OF MISERY AND SUFFERING, SITS A HORRID SHIP OF ILL INTENT.
HAPPINESS! I HATE IT! IT GIVES ME SUCH A HEADACHE!

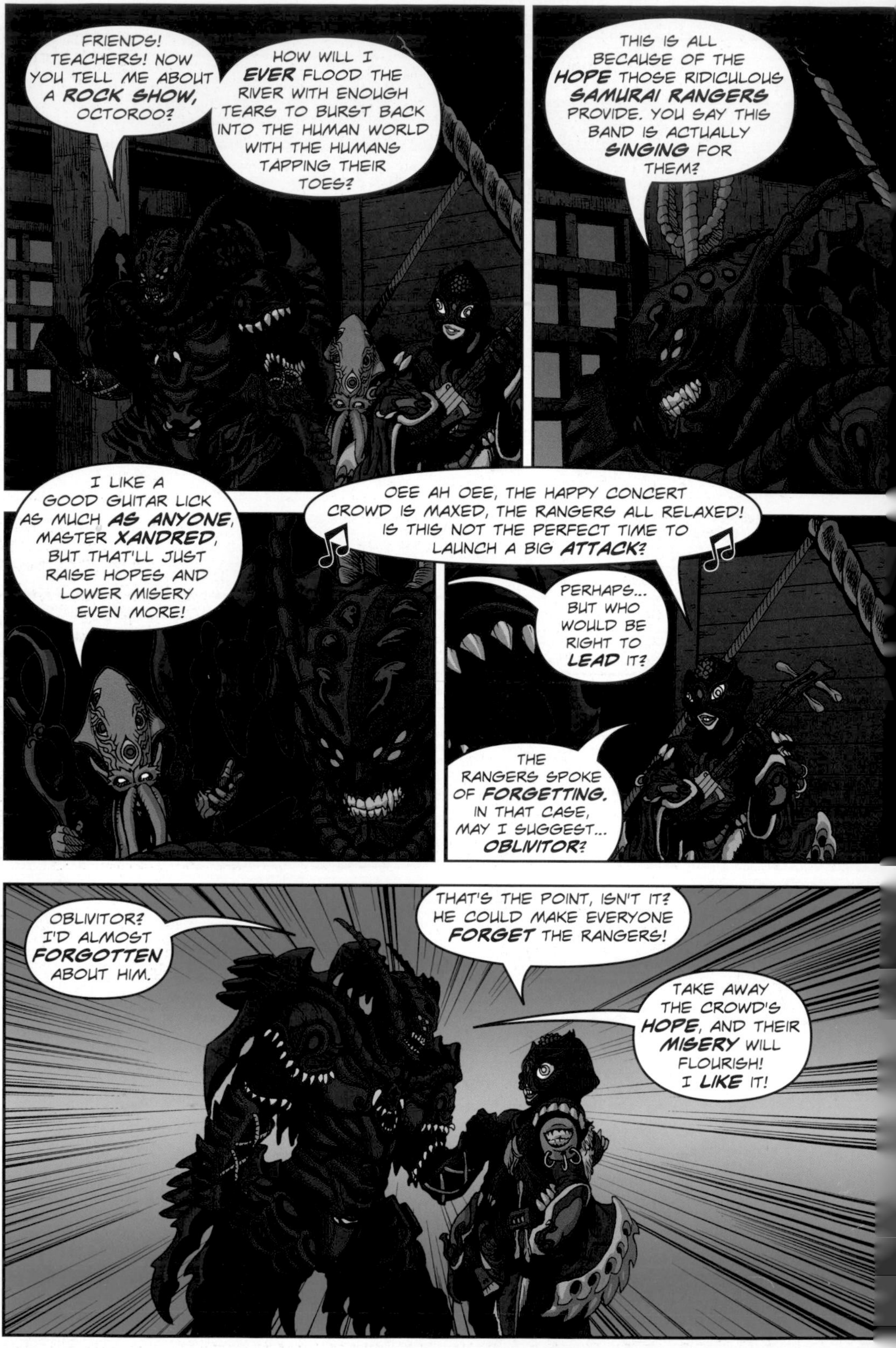
FRIENDS! TEACHERS! NOW YOU TELL ME ABOUT A ROCK SHOW, OCTOROO?
HOW WILL I EVER FLOOD THE RIVER WITH ENOUGH TEARS TO BURST BACK INTO THE HUMAN WORLD WITH THE HUMANS TAPPING THEIR TOES?
THIS IS ALL BECAUSE OF THE HOPE THOSE RIDICULOUS SAMURAI RANGERS PROVIDE. YOU SAY THIS BAND IS ACTUALLY SINGING FOR THEM?
I LIKE A GOOD GUITAR LICK AS MUCH AS ANYONE, MASTER XANDRED, BUT THAT'LL JUST RAISE HOPES AND LOWER MISERY EVEN MORE!
OEE AH OEE, THE HAPPY CONCERT CROWD IS MAXED, THE RANGERS ALL RELAXED! IS THIS NOT THE PERFECT TIME TO LAUNCH A BIG ATTACK?
PERHAPS... BUT WHO WOULD BE RIGHT TO LEAD IT?
THE RANGERS SPOKE OF FORGETTING. IN THAT CASE, MAY I SUGGEST... OBLIVITOR?
OBLIVITOR? I'D ALMOST FORGOTTEN ABOUT HIM.
THAT'S THE POINT, ISN'T IT? HE COULD MAKE EVERYONE FORGET THE RANGERS!
TAKE AWAY THE CROWD'S HOPE, AND THEIR MISERY WILL FLOURISH! I LIKE IT!

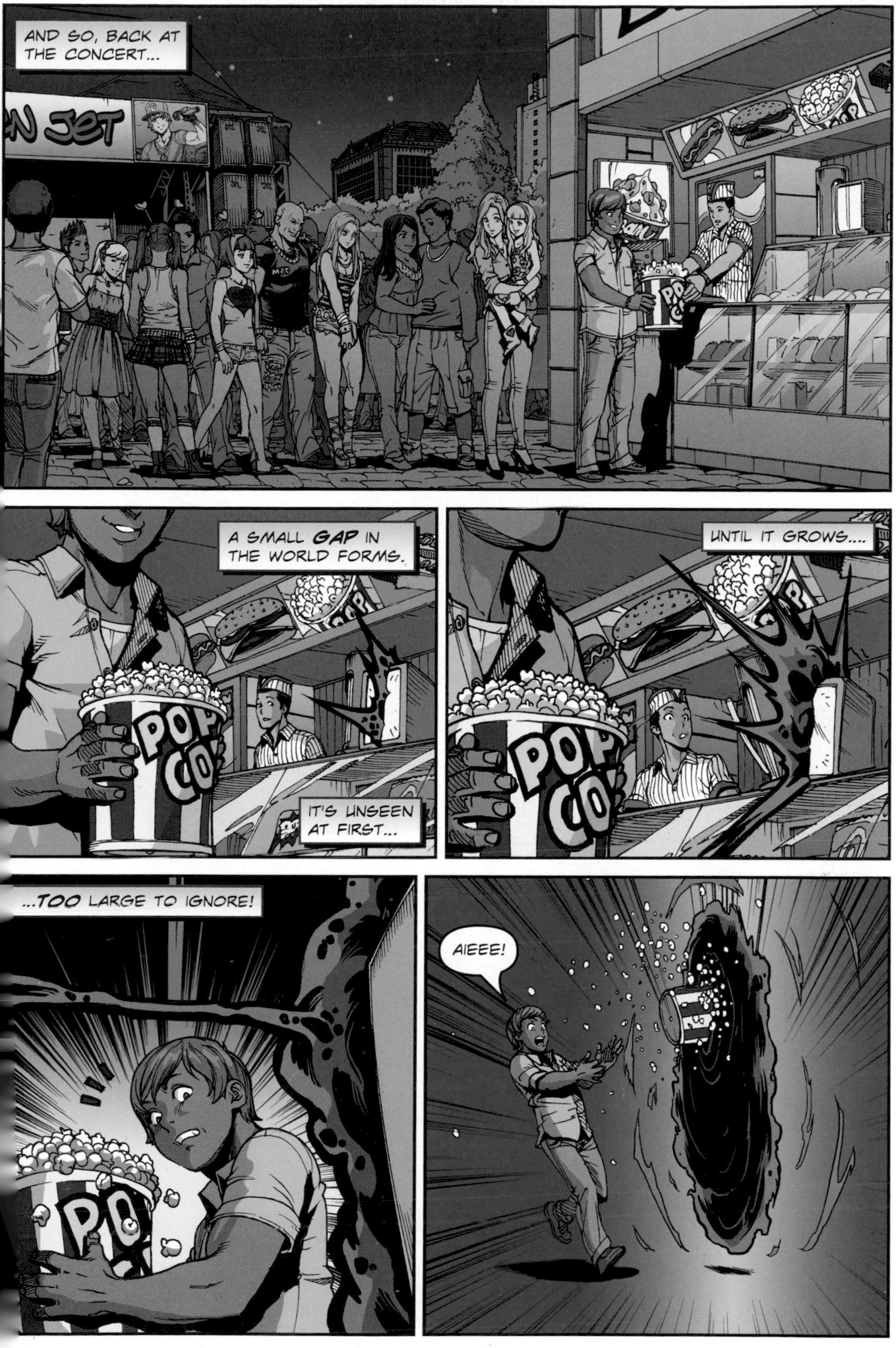
AND SO, BACK AT THE CONCERT...
A SMALL GAP IN THE WORLD FORMS.
IT'S UNSEEN AT FIRST...
UNTIL IT GROWS....
...TOO LARGE TO IGNORE!
AIEEE!

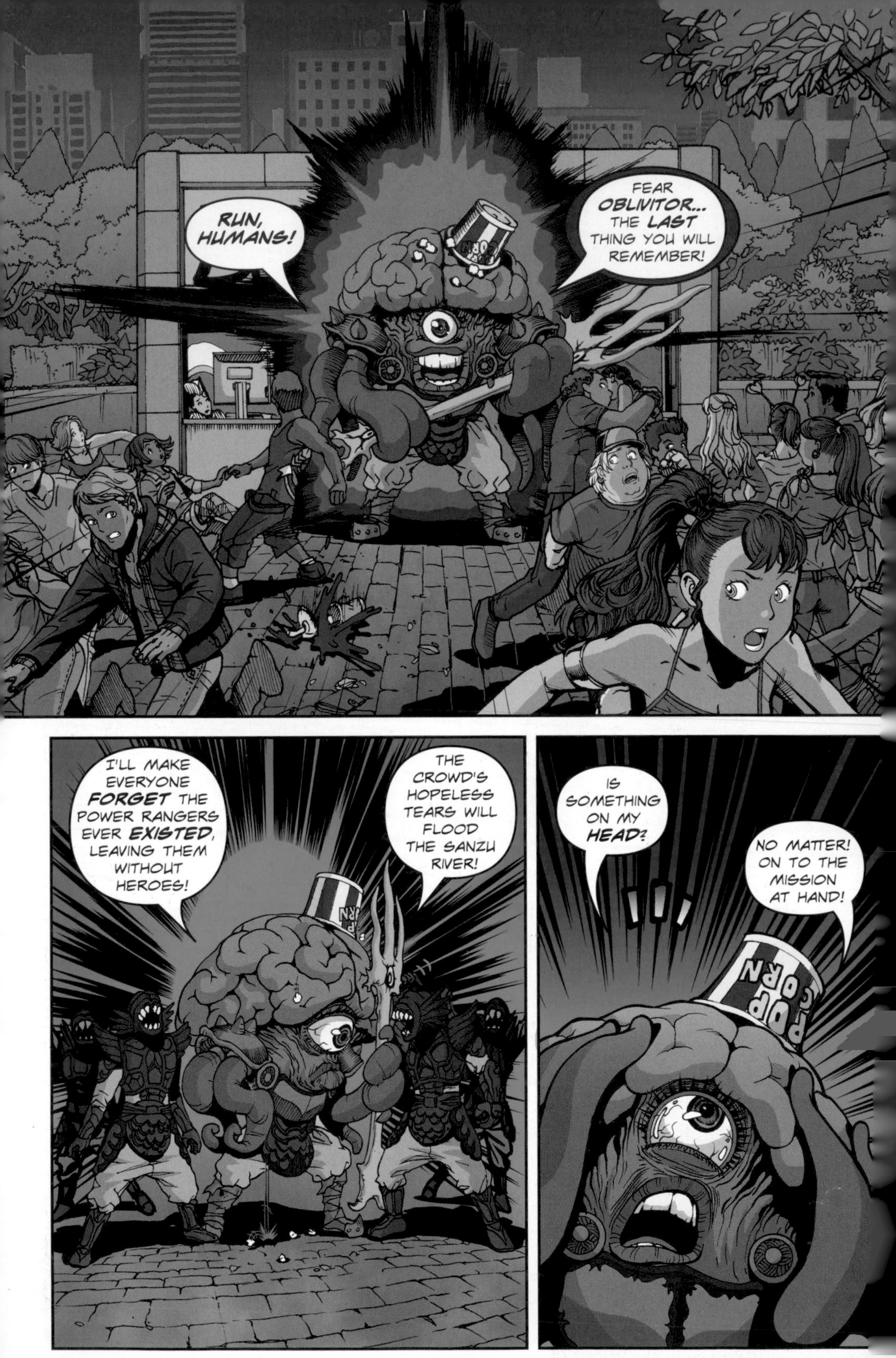
RUN, HUMANS!
FEAR OBLIVITOR... THE LAST THING YOU WILL REMEMBER!
I'LL MAKE EVERYONE FORGET THE POWER RANGERS EVER EXISTED, LEAVING THEM WITHOUT HEROES!
THE CROWD'S HOPELESS TEARS WILL FLOOD THE SANZU RIVER!
IS SOMETHING ON MY HEAD?
NO MATTER! ON TO THE MISSION AT HAND!
POP CORN

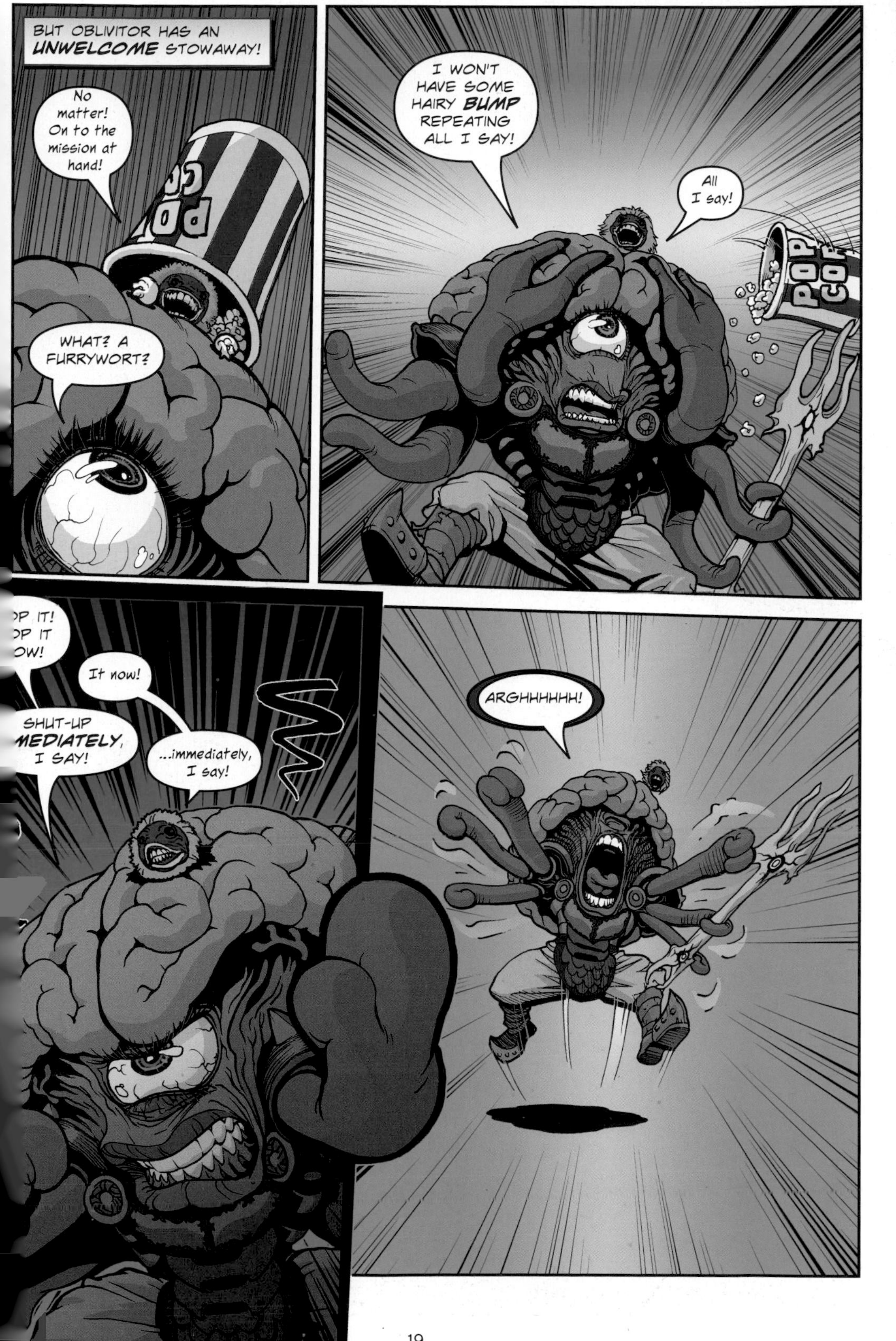
BUT OBLIVITOR HAS AN UNWELCOME STOWAWAY!
No matter! On to the mission at hand!
WHAT? A FURRYWORT?
I WON'T HAVE SOME HAIRY BUMP REPEATING ALL I SAY!
All I say!
IT!
IT
OW!
It now!
SHUT-UP
MEDIATELY, I SAY!
...immediately, I say!
ARGHHHHHH!

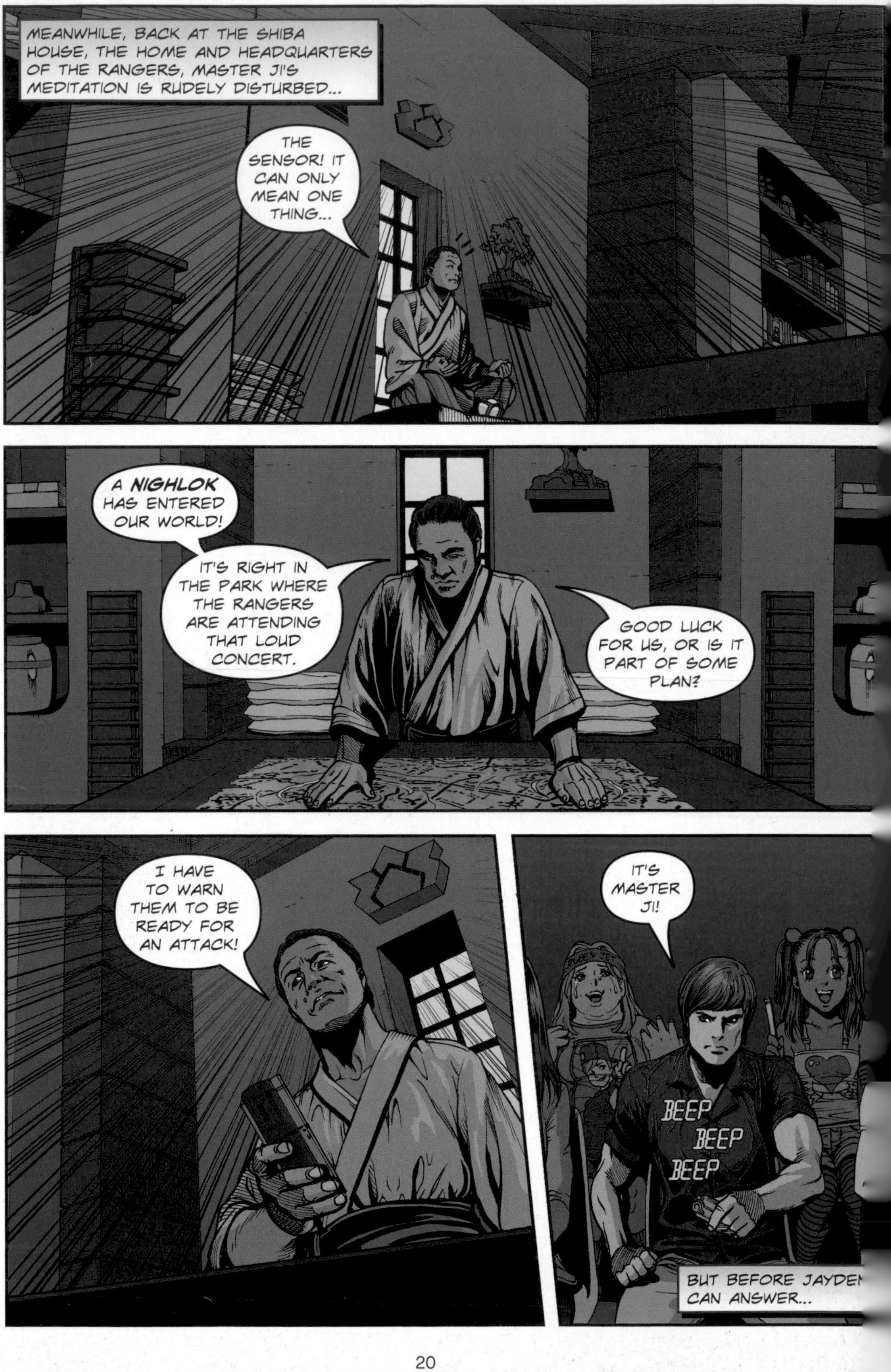
MEANWHILE, BACK AT THE SHIBA HOUSE, THE HOME AND HEADQUARTERS OF THE RANGERS, MASTER JI'S MEDITATION IS RUDELY DISTURBED...
THE SENSOR! IT CAN ONLY MEAN ONE THING...
A NIGHLOK HAS ENTERED OUR WORLD!
IT'S RIGHT IN THE PARK WHERE THE RANGERS ARE ATTENDING THAT LOUD CONCERT.
GOOD LUCK FOR US, OR IS IT PART OF SOME PLAN?
I HAVE TO WARN THEM TO BE READY FOR AN ATTACK!
IT'S MASTER JI!
BEEP
BEEP
BEEP
BUT BEFORE JAYDEN CAN ANSWER...

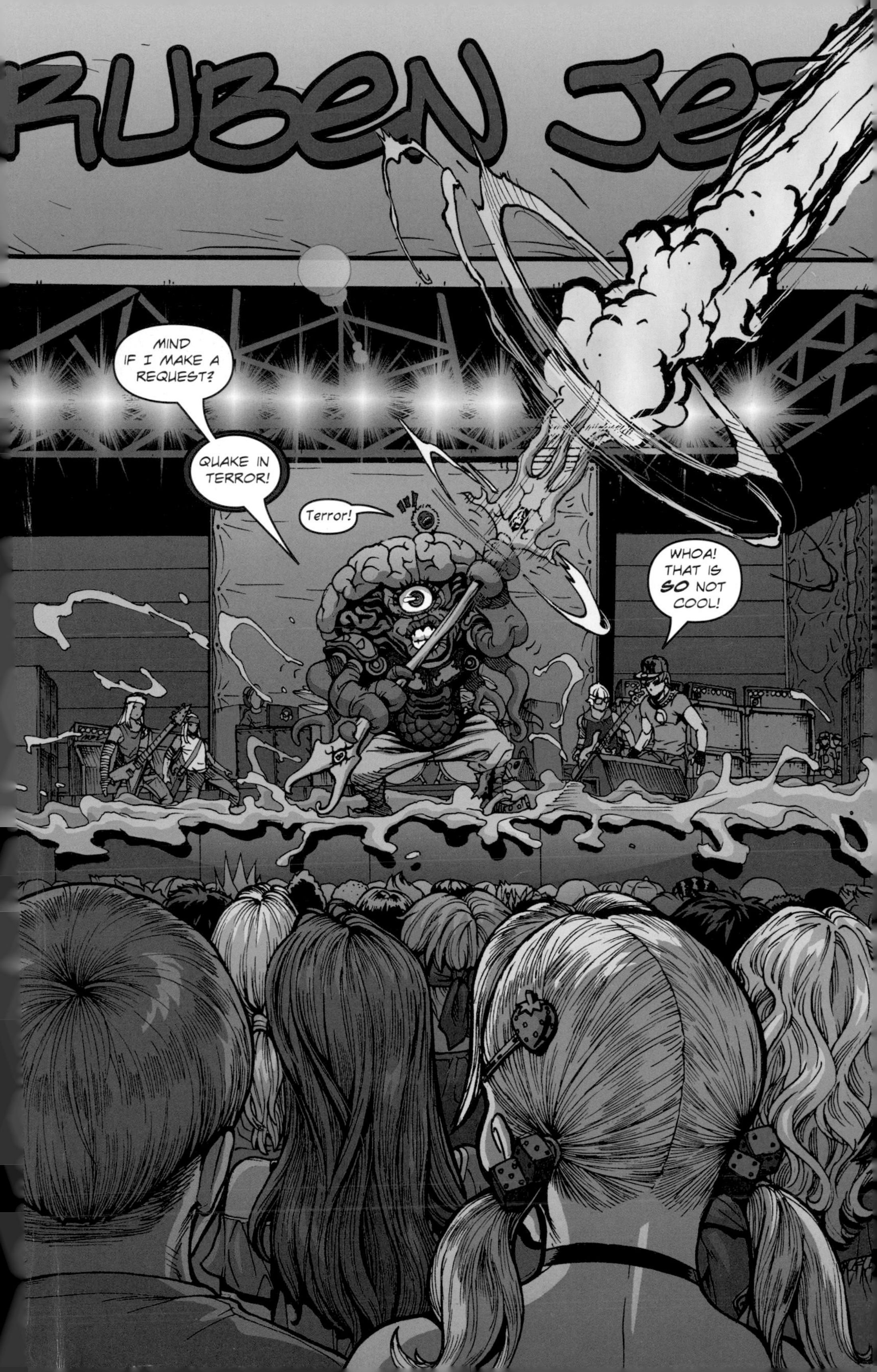
RUBEN JE
MIND IF I MAKE A REQUEST?
QUAKE IN TERROR!
Terror!
WHOA! THAT IS SO NOT COOL!

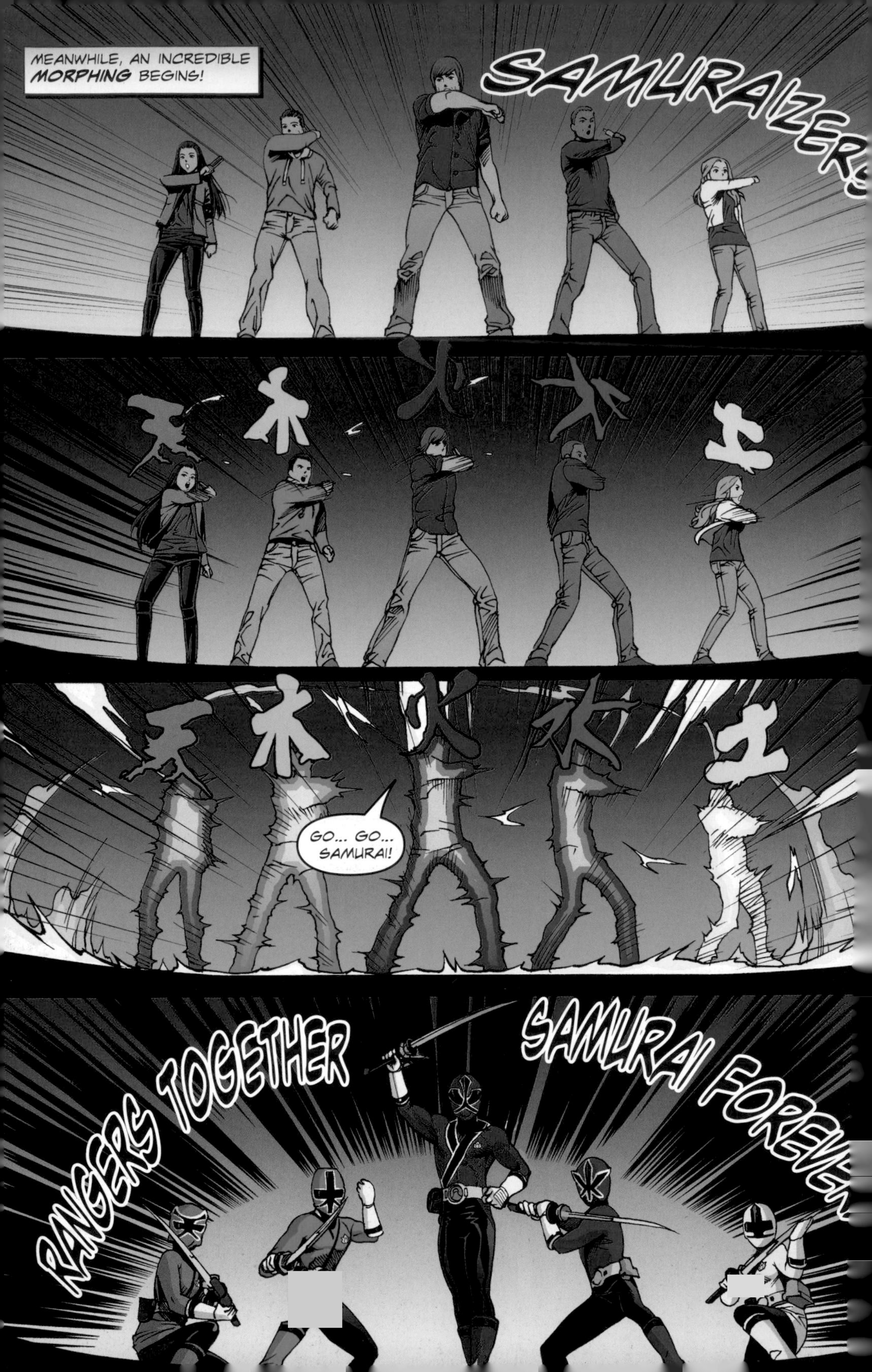
MEANWHILE, AN INCREDIBLE MORPHING BEGINS!
SAMURAIZERS
天 木 火 水 土
天 木 火 水 土
GO... GO... SAMURAI!
RANGERS TOGETHER
SAMURAI FOREVE

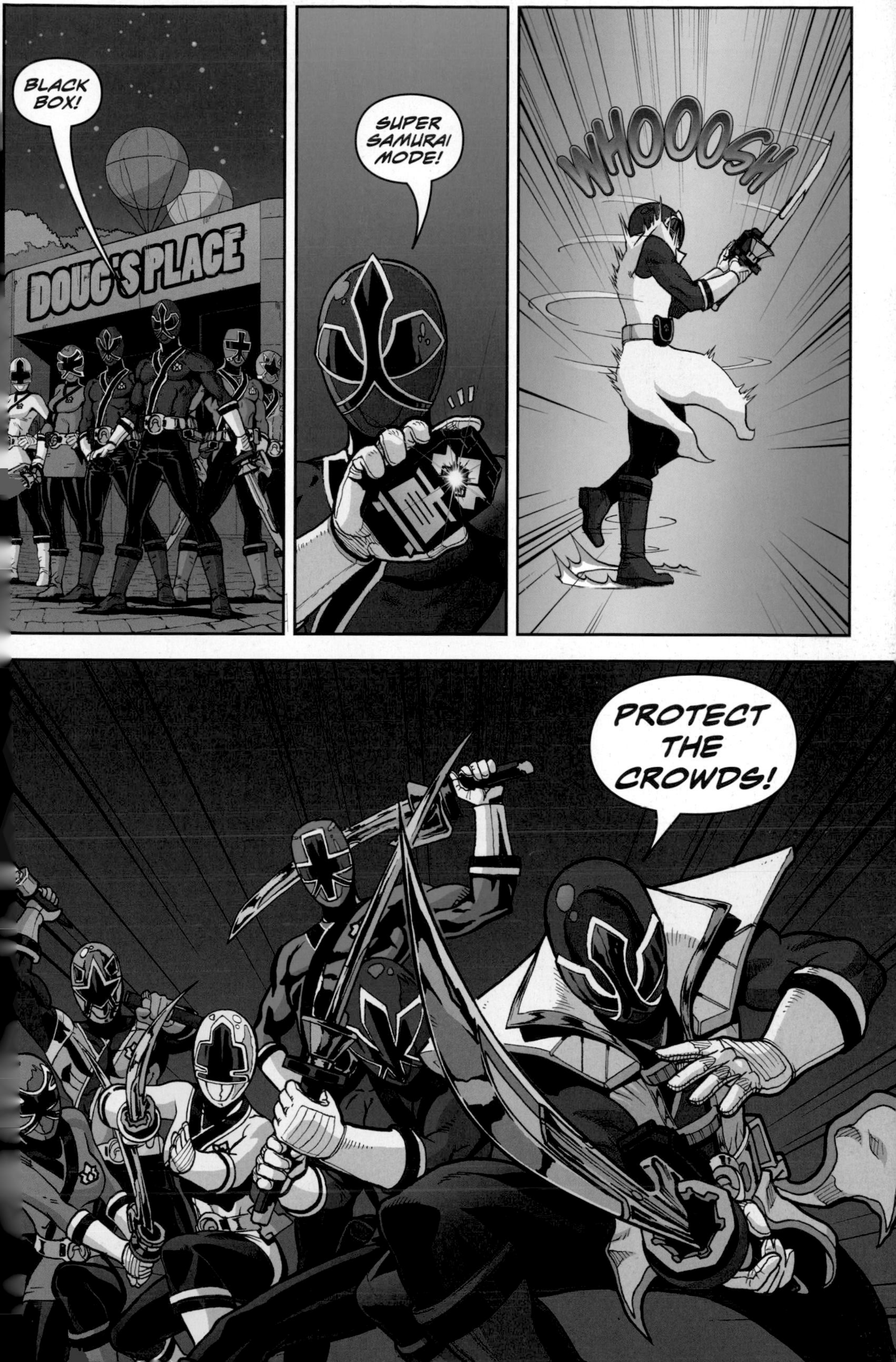
BLACK BOX!
DOUG'S PLACE
SUPER SAMURAI MODE!
WHOOOSH
PROTECT THE CROWDS!

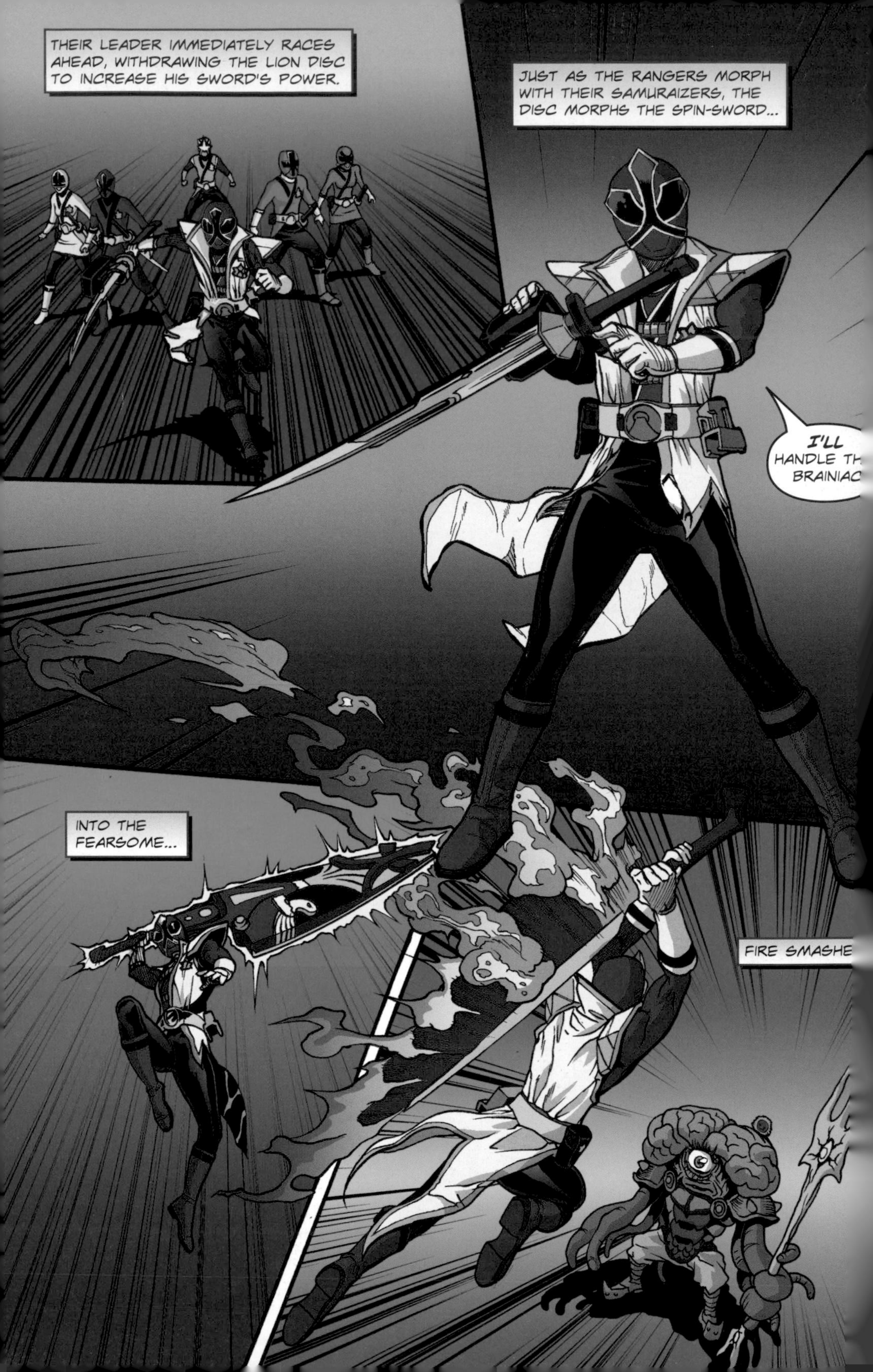
THEIR LEADER IMMEDIATELY RACES AHEAD, WITHDRAWING THE LION DISC TO INCREASE HIS SWORD'S POWER.
JUST AS THE RANGERS MORPH WITH THEIR SAMURAIZERS, THE DISC MORPHS THE SPIN-SWORD...
I'LL HANDLE TH
BRAINIAC
INTO THE FEARSOME...
FIRE SMASHE

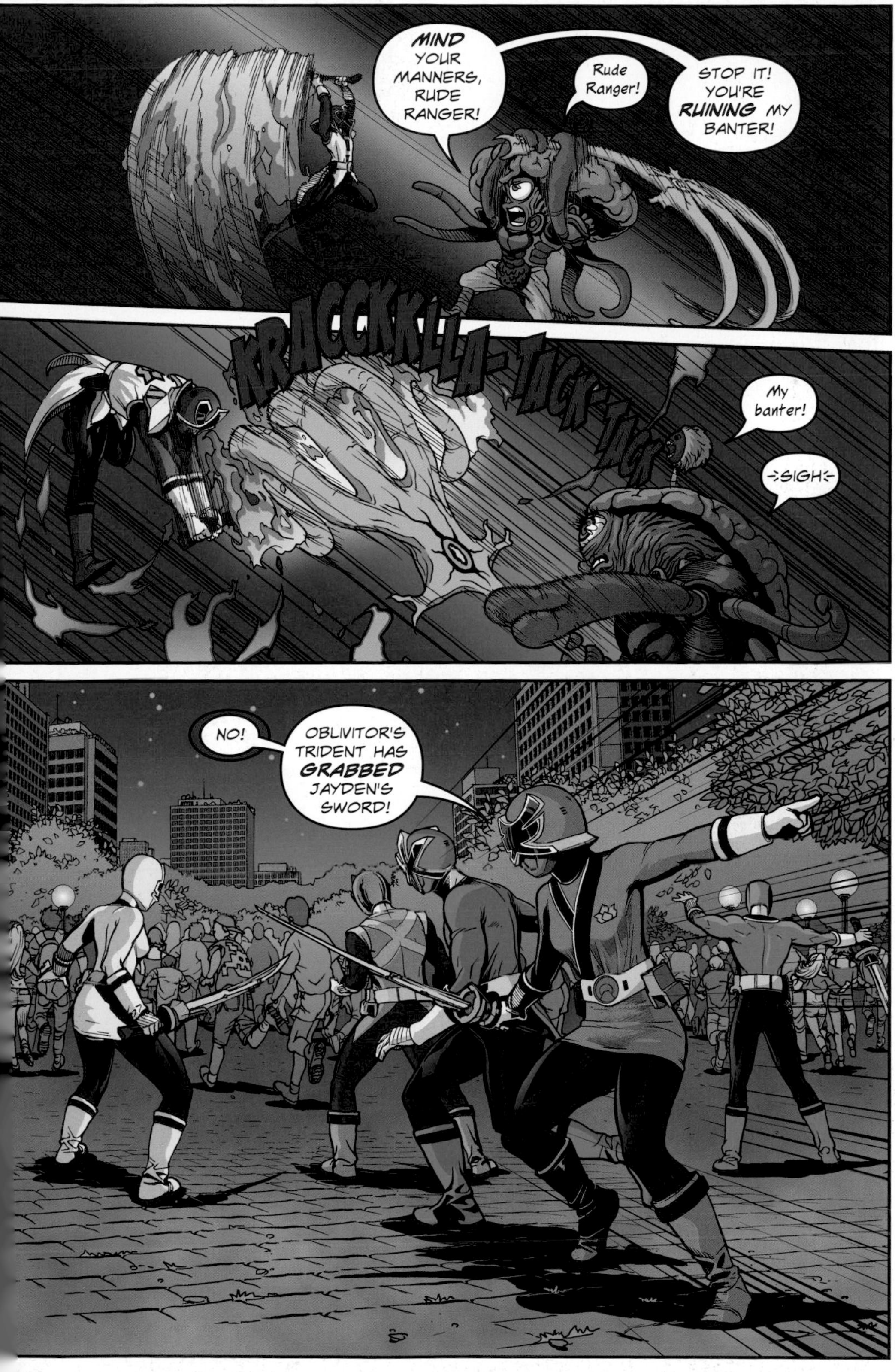
MIND YOUR MANNERS, RUDE RANGER!
Rude Ranger!
STOP IT! YOU'RE RUINING MY BANTER!
KRACCKKLLA-TACK-TACK
My banter!
SIGH
NO!
OBLIVITOR'S TRIDENT HAS GRABBED JAYDEN'S SWORD!

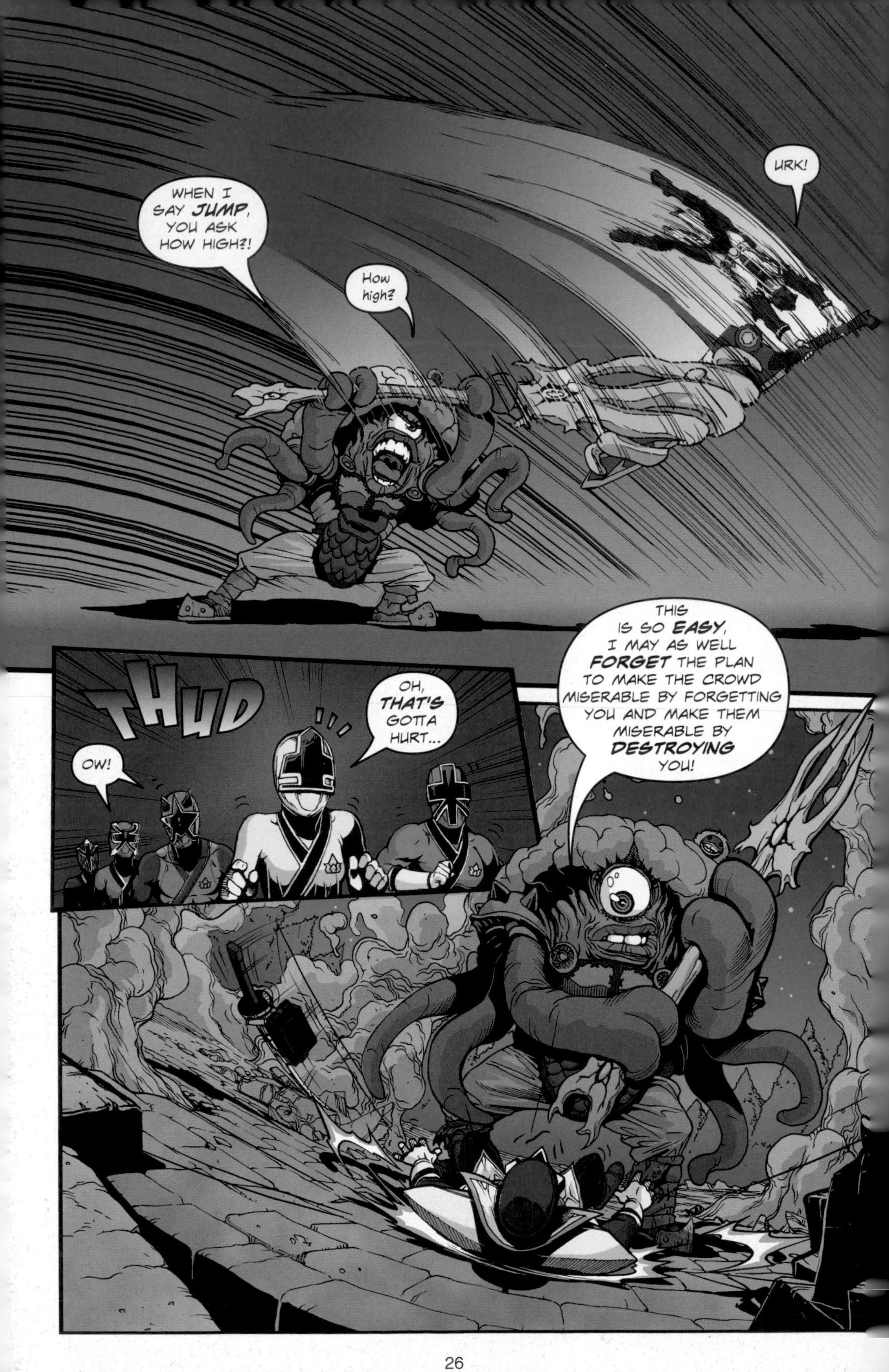
WHEN I SAY JUMP, YOU ASK HOW HIGH?!
How high?
URK!
THUD
OW!
OH, THAT'S GOTTA HURT...
THIS IS SO EASY, I MAY AS WELL FORGET THE PLAN TO MAKE THE CROWD MISERABLE BY FORGETTING YOU AND MAKE THEM MISERABLE BY DESTROYING YOU!

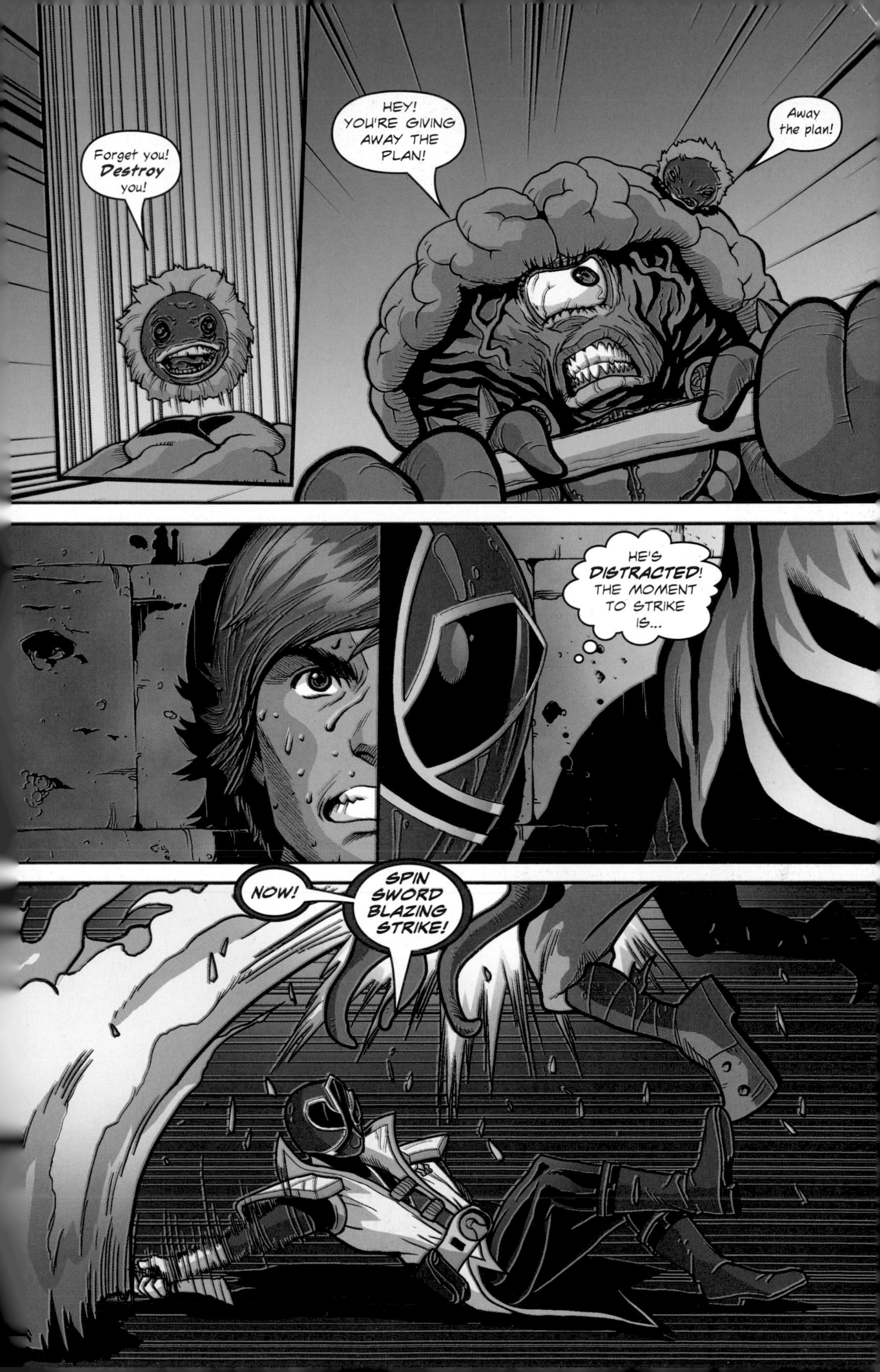
Forget you! Destroy you!
HEY! YOU'RE GIVING AWAY THE PLAN!
Away the plan!
HE'S DISTRACTED! THE MOMENT TO STRIKE IS...
NOW!
SPIN SWORD BLAZING STRIKE!

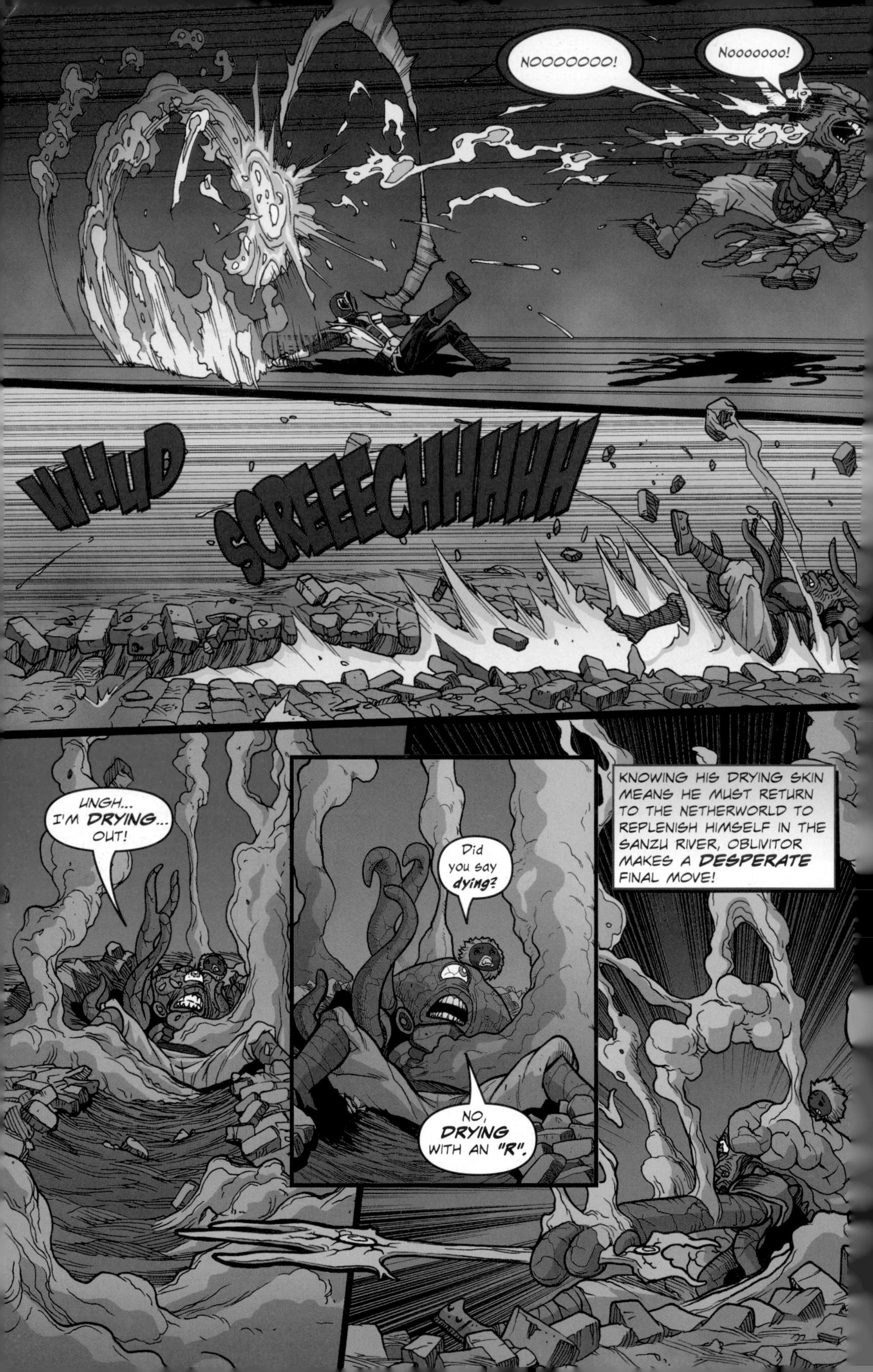
NOOOOOOO!
Nooooooo!
WHUD
SCREEECHHHHH
UNGH... I'M DRYING... OUT!
Did you say dying?
NO, DRYING WITH AN "R".
KNOWING HIS DRYING SKIN MEANS HE MUST RETURN TO THE NETHERWORLD TO REPLENISH HIMSELF IN THE SANZU RIVER, OBLIVITOR MAKES A DESPERATE FINAL MOVE!

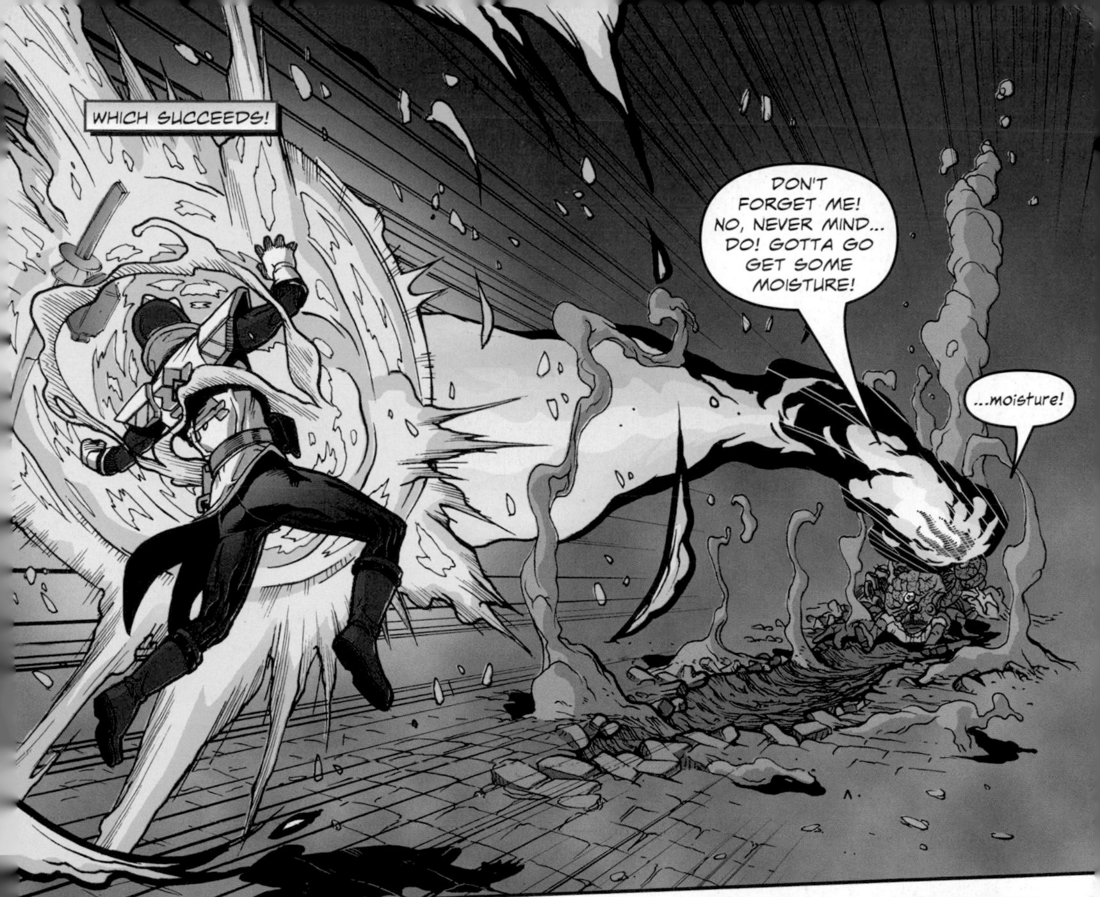
WHICH SUCCEEDS!
DON'T FORGET ME! NO, NEVER MIND... DO! GOTTA GO GET SOME MOISTURE!
...moisture!

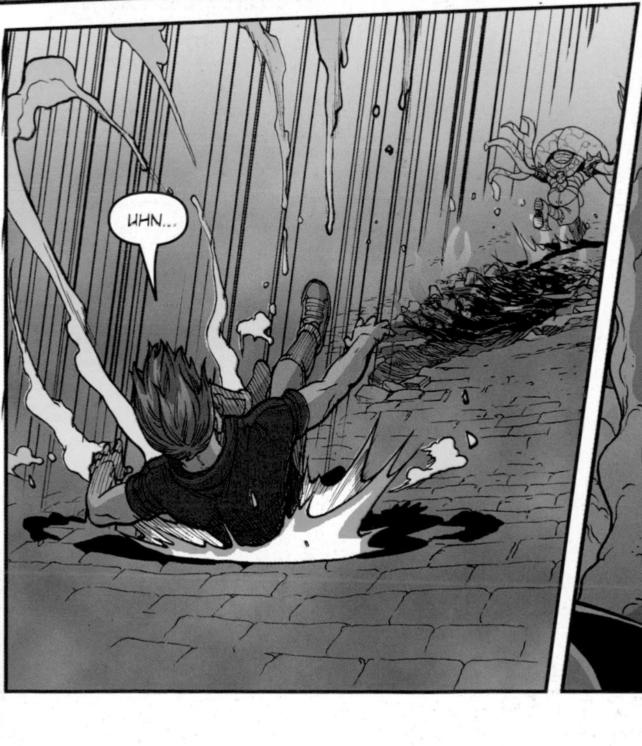
UHN...

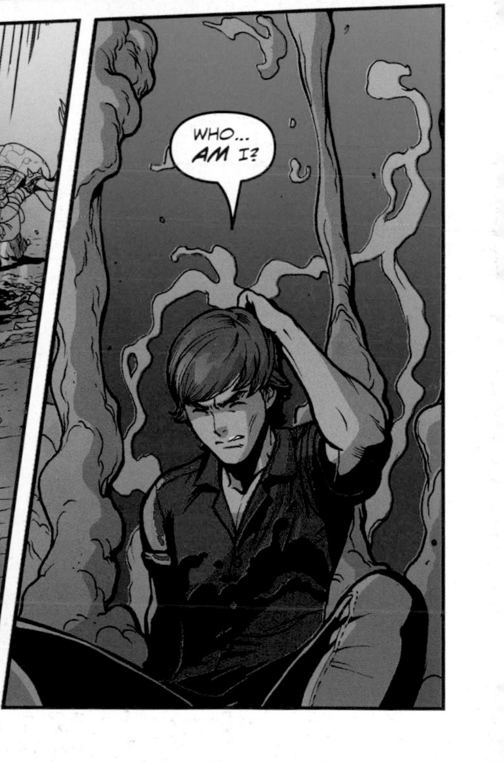
WHO... AM I?

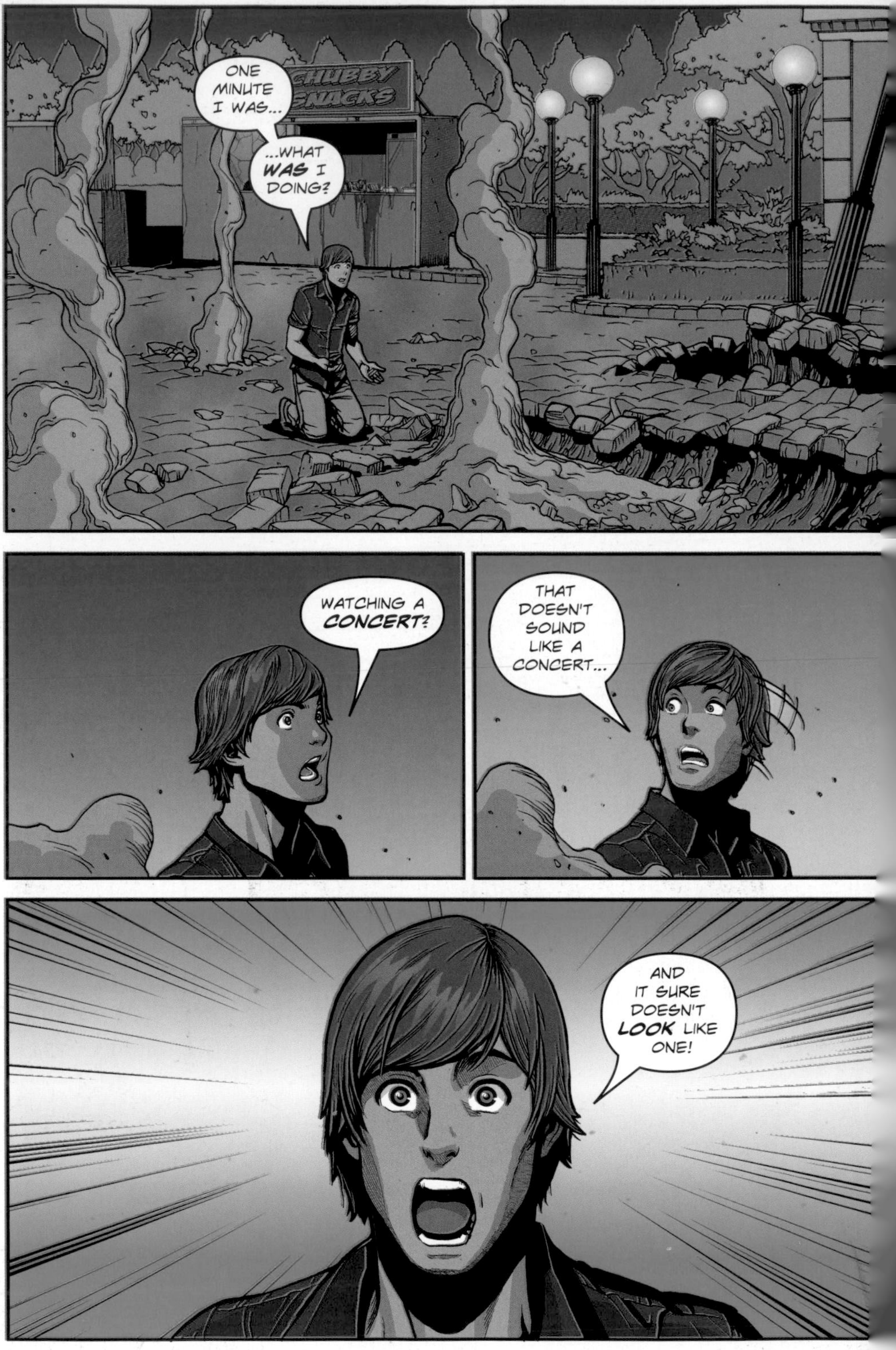
CHUBBY SNACKS
ONE MINUTE I WAS...
...WHAT WAS I DOING?
WATCHING A CONCERT?
THAT DOESN'T SOUND LIKE A CONCERT...
AND IT SURE DOESN'T LOOK LIKE ONE!

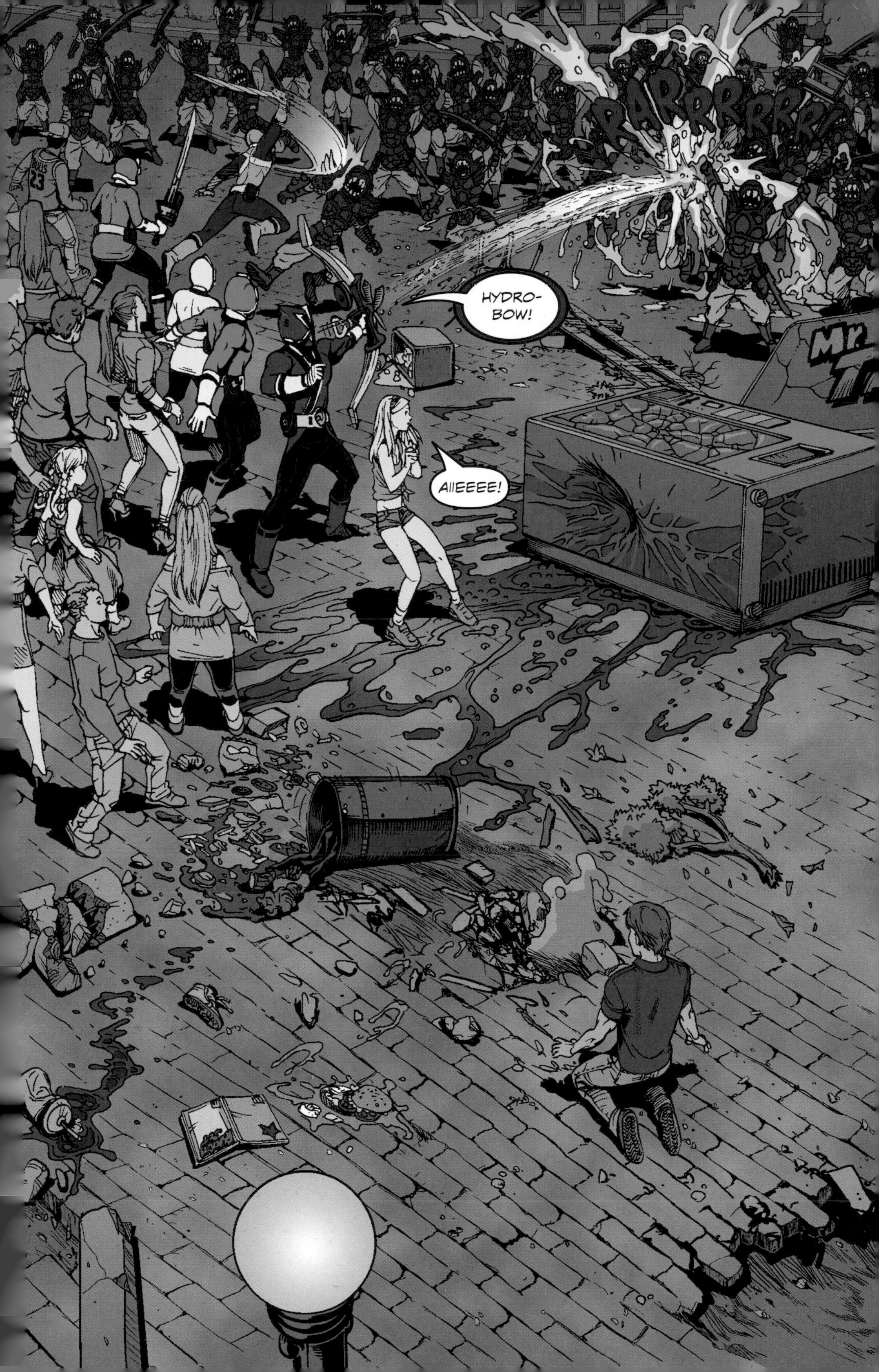
RARRRRRR
HYDRO-
BOW!
AIIEEEE!

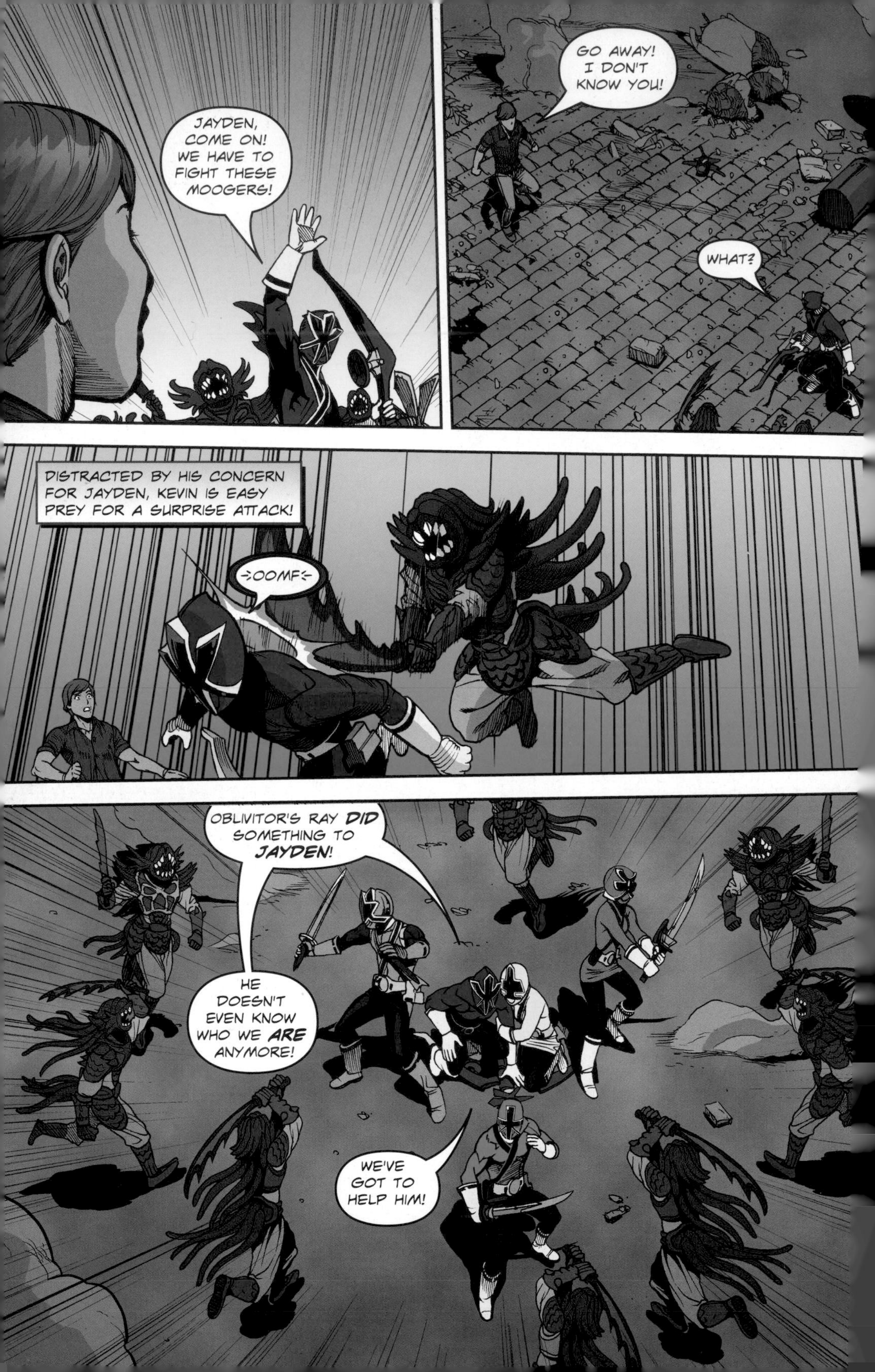
JAYDEN, COME ON! WE HAVE TO FIGHT THESE MOOGERS!
GO AWAY! I DON'T KNOW YOU!
WHAT?
DISTRACTED BY HIS CONCERN FOR JAYDEN, KEVIN IS EASY PREY FOR A SURPRISE ATTACK!
-OOMF-
OBLIVITOR'S RAY DID SOMETHING TO JAYDEN!
HE DOESN'T EVEN KNOW WHO WE ARE ANYMORE!
WE'VE GOT TO HELP HIM!

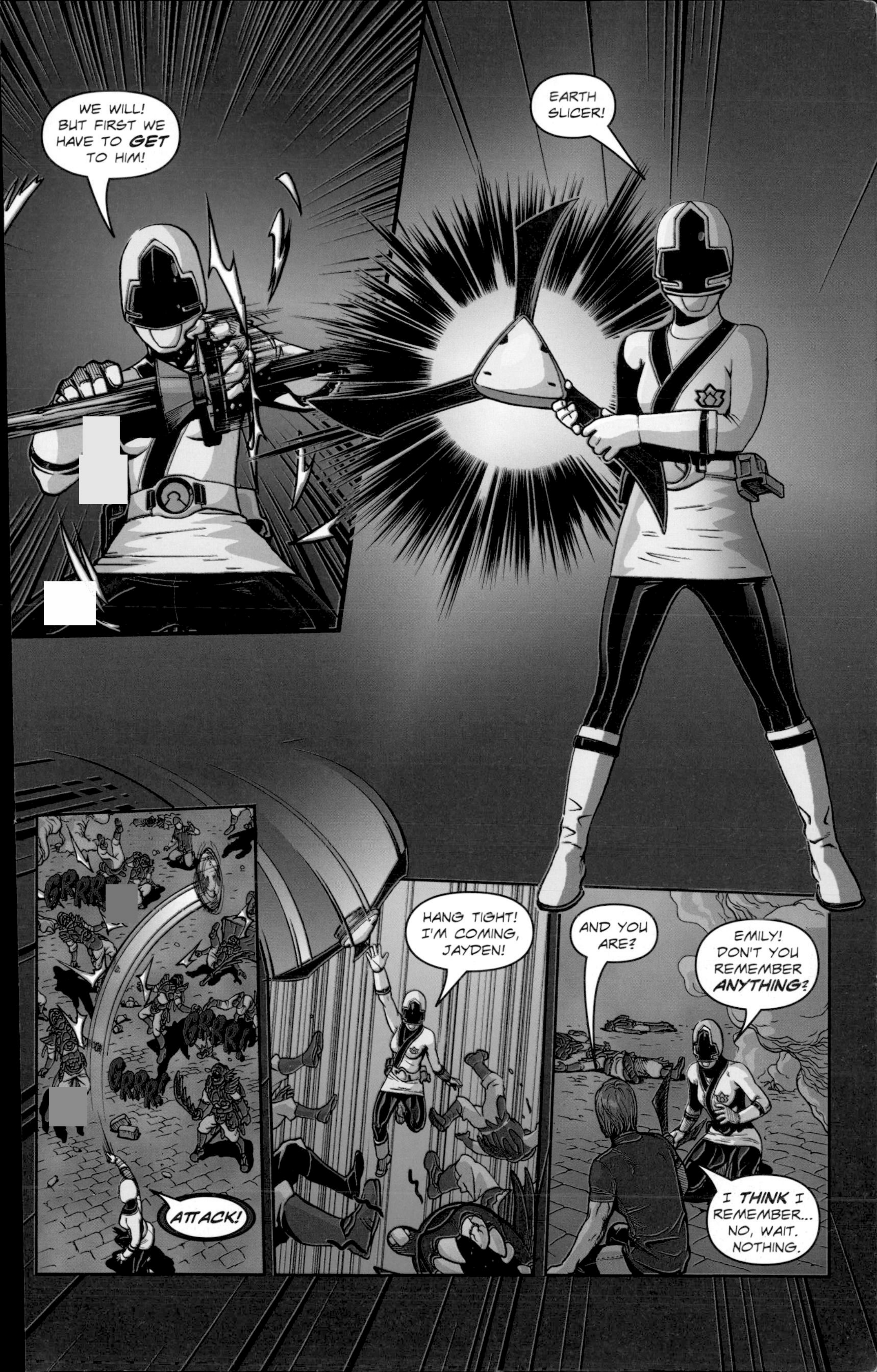
WE WILL! BUT FIRST WE HAVE TO GET TO HIM!
EARTH SLICER!
ATTACK!
HANG TIGHT! I'M COMING, JAYDEN!
AND YOU ARE?
EMILY! DON'T YOU REMEMBER ANYTHING?
I THINK I REMEMBER... NO, WAIT. NOTHING.

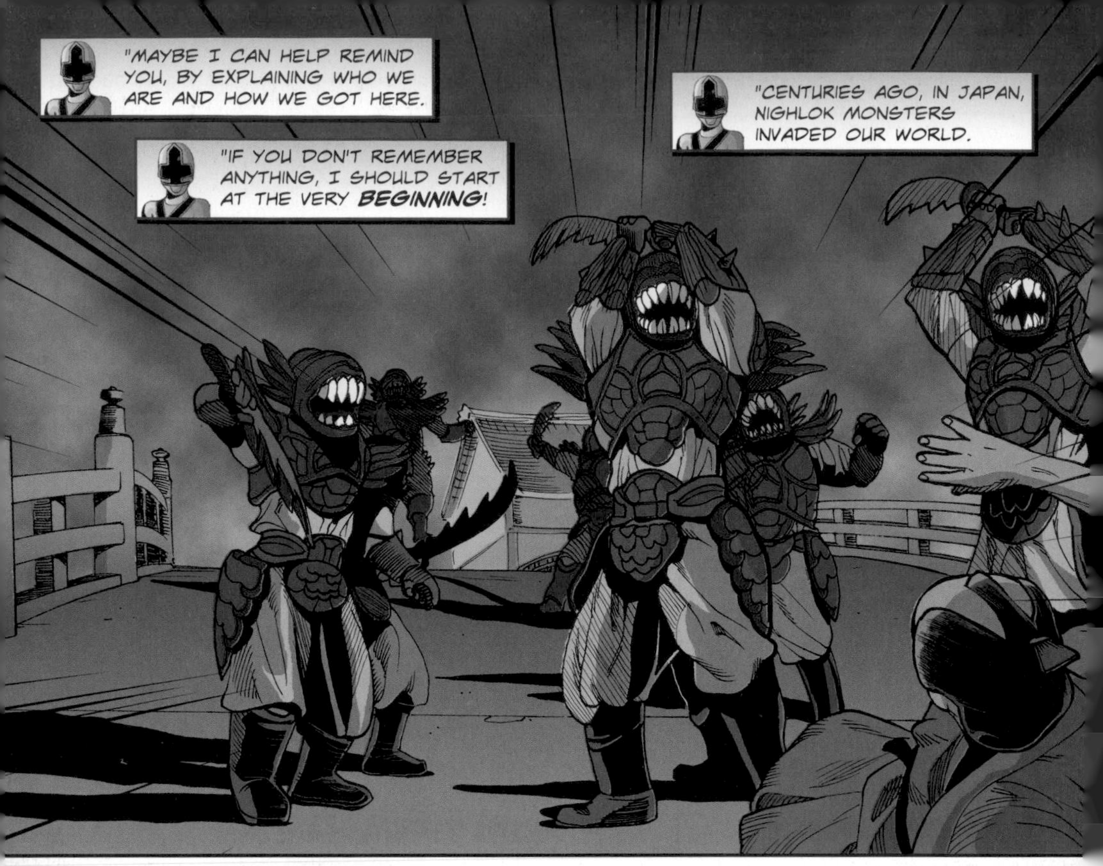
"MAYBE I CAN HELP REMIND YOU, BY EXPLAINING WHO WE ARE AND HOW WE GOT HERE.
"IF YOU DON'T REMEMBER ANYTHING, I SHOULD START AT THE VERY BEGINNING!
"CENTURIES AGO, IN JAPAN, NIGHLOK MONSTERS INVADED OUR WORLD.

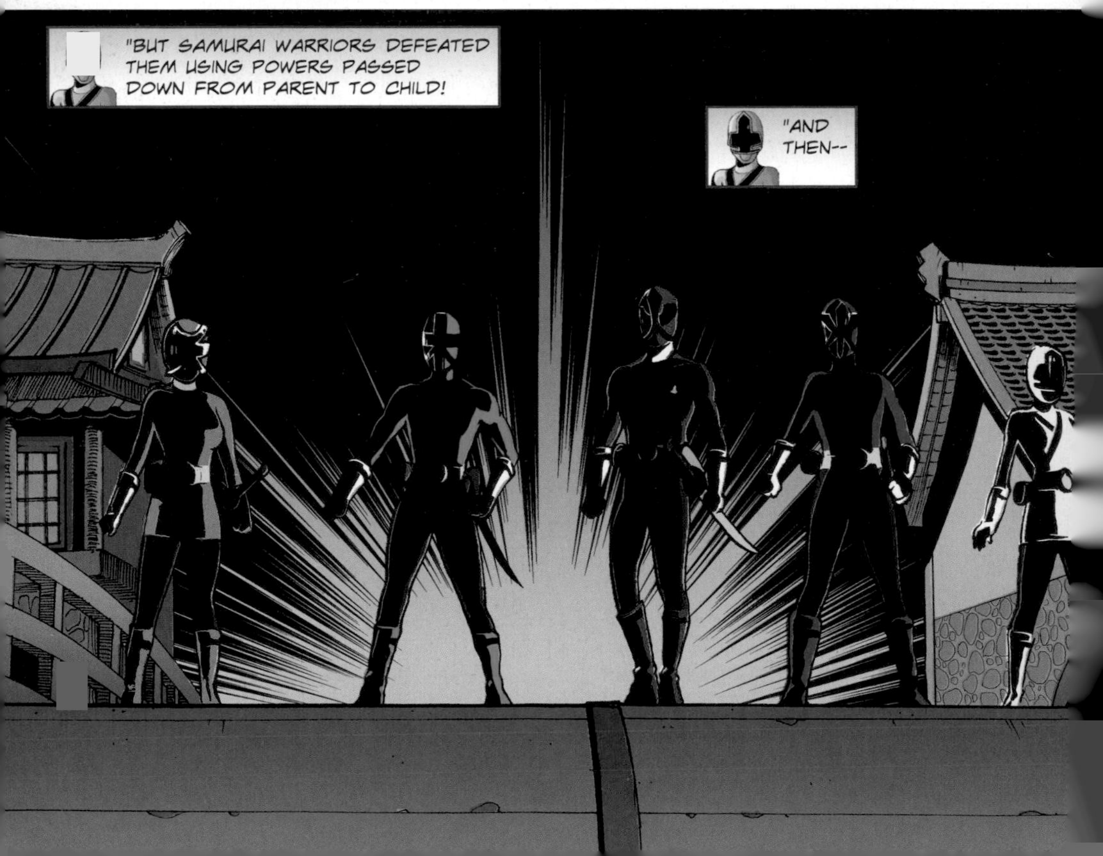
"BUT SAMURAI WARRIORS DEFEATED THEM USING POWERS PASSED DOWN FROM PARENT TO CHILD!
"AND THEN--

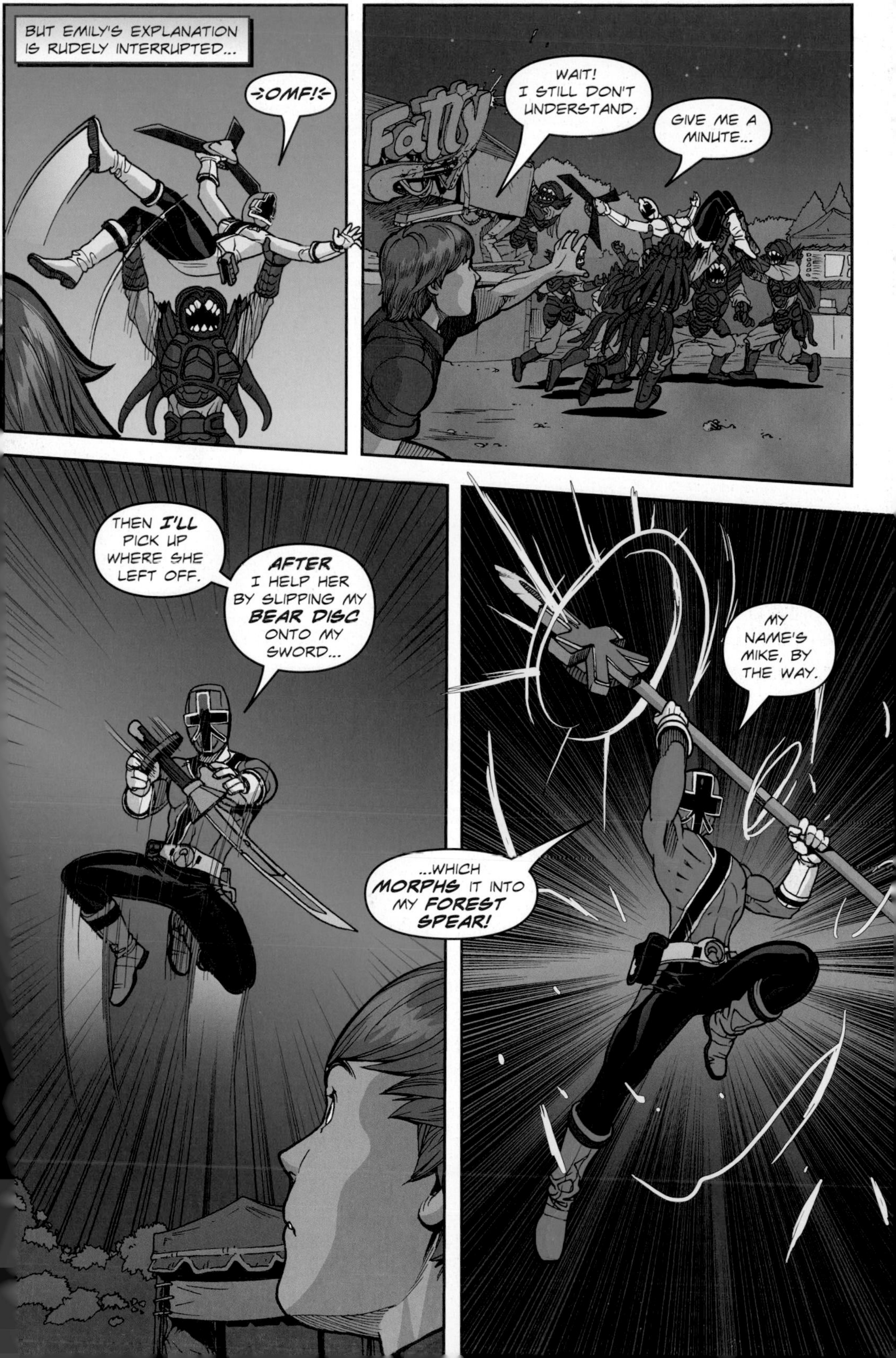
BUT EMILY'S EXPLANATION IS RUDELY INTERRUPTED...
OMF!
WAIT! I STILL DON'T UNDERSTAND.
GIVE ME A MINUTE...
THEN I'LL PICK UP WHERE SHE LEFT OFF.
AFTER I HELP HER BY SLIPPING MY BEAR DISC ONTO MY SWORD...
MY NAME'S MIKE, BY THE WAY.
...WHICH MORPHS IT INTO MY FOREST SPEAR!

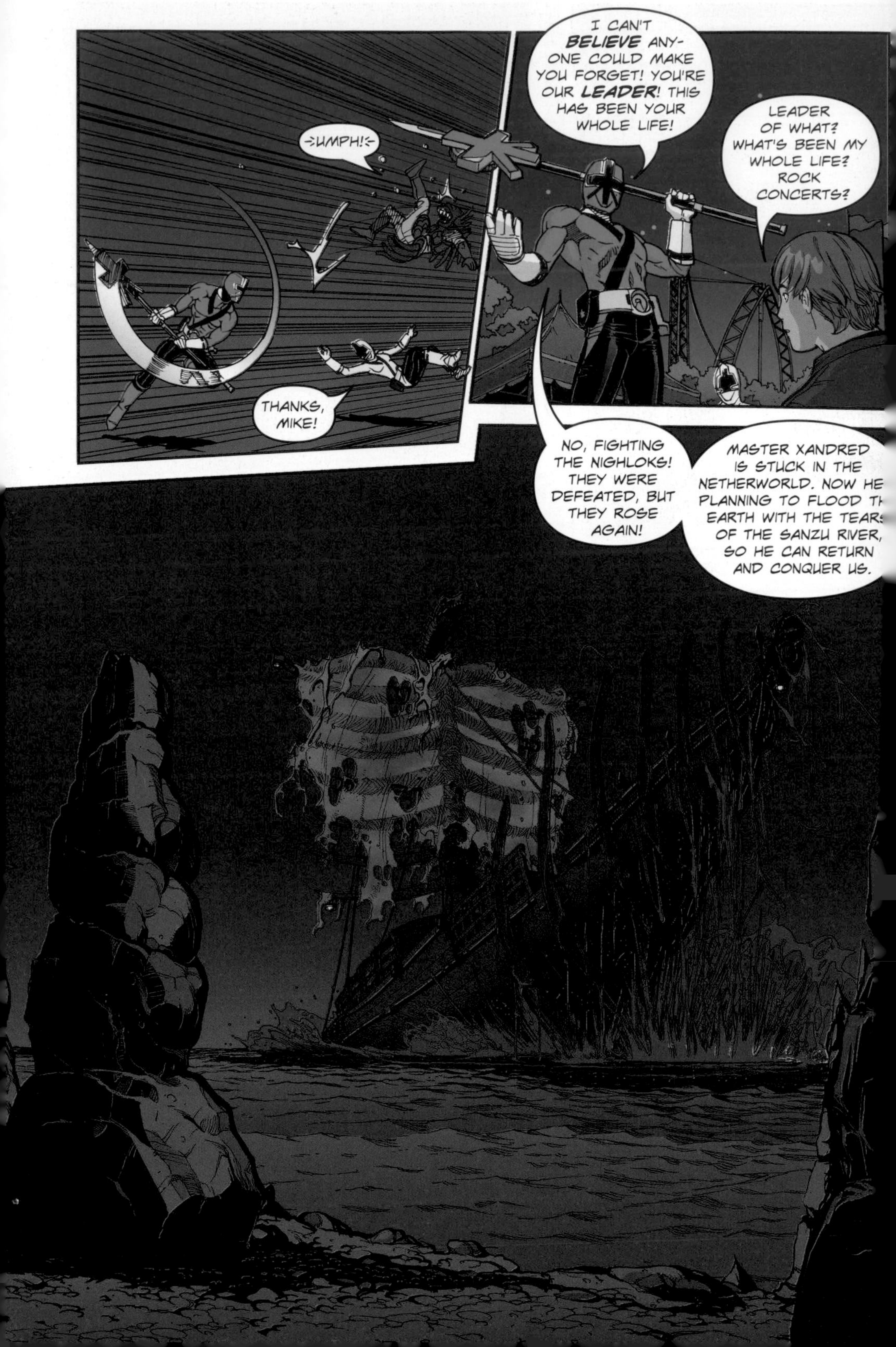

-UMPH!-
THANKS, MIKE!
I CAN'T BELIEVE ANYONE COULD MAKE YOU FORGET! YOU'RE OUR LEADER! THIS HAS BEEN YOUR WHOLE LIFE!
LEADER OF WHAT? WHAT'S BEEN MY WHOLE LIFE? ROCK CONCERTS?
NO, FIGHTING THE NIGHLOKS! THEY WERE DEFEATED, BUT THEY ROSE AGAIN!
MASTER XANDRED IS STUCK IN THE NETHERWORLD. NOW HE PLANNING TO FLOOD TH EARTH WITH THE TEARS OF THE SANZU RIVER, SO HE CAN RETURN AND CONQUER US.

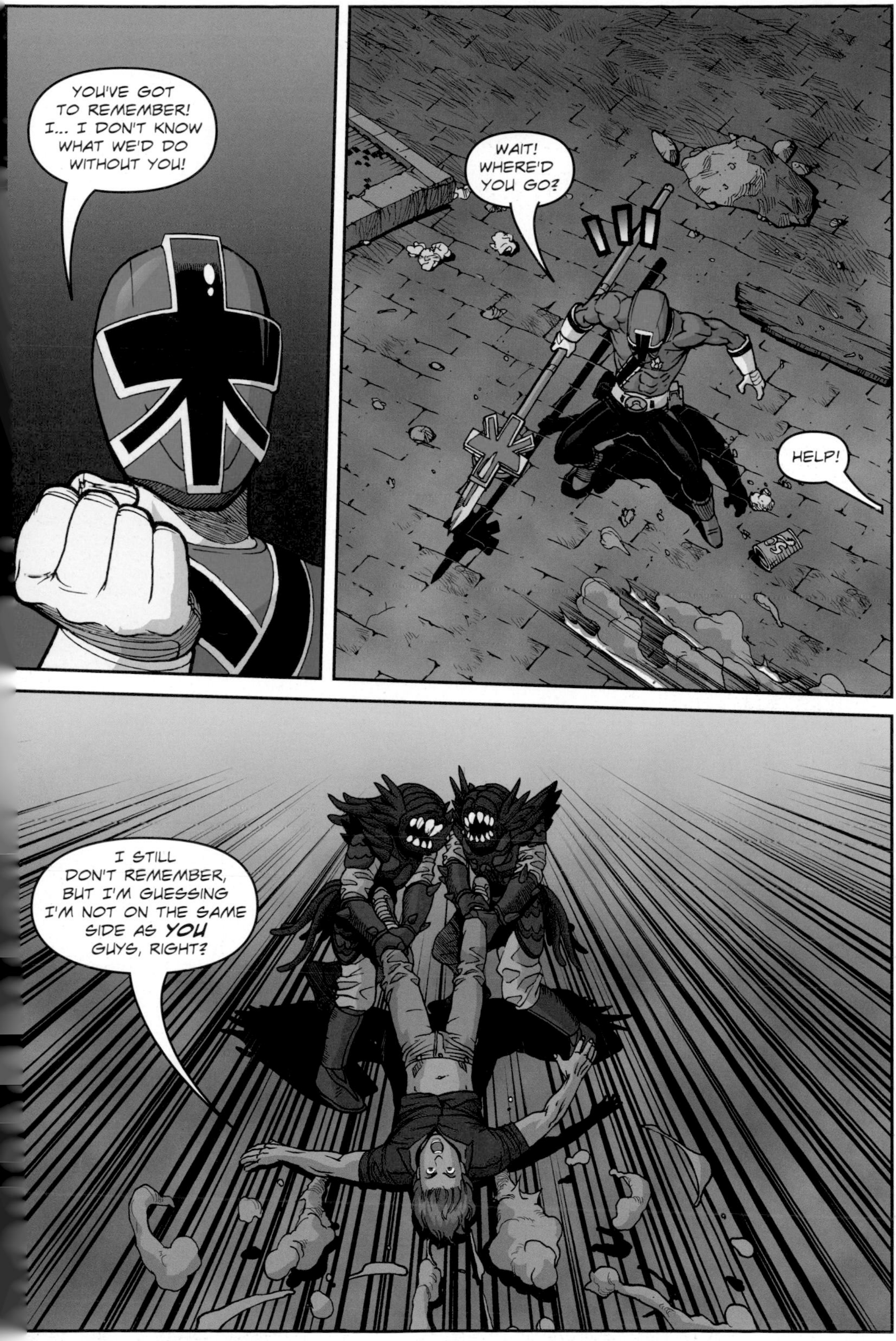
YOU'VE GOT TO REMEMBER! I... I DON'T KNOW WHAT WE'D DO WITHOUT YOU!
WAIT! WHERE'D YOU GO?
HELP!
I STILL DON'T REMEMBER, BUT I'M GUESSING I'M NOT ON THE SAME SIDE AS YOU GUYS, RIGHT?

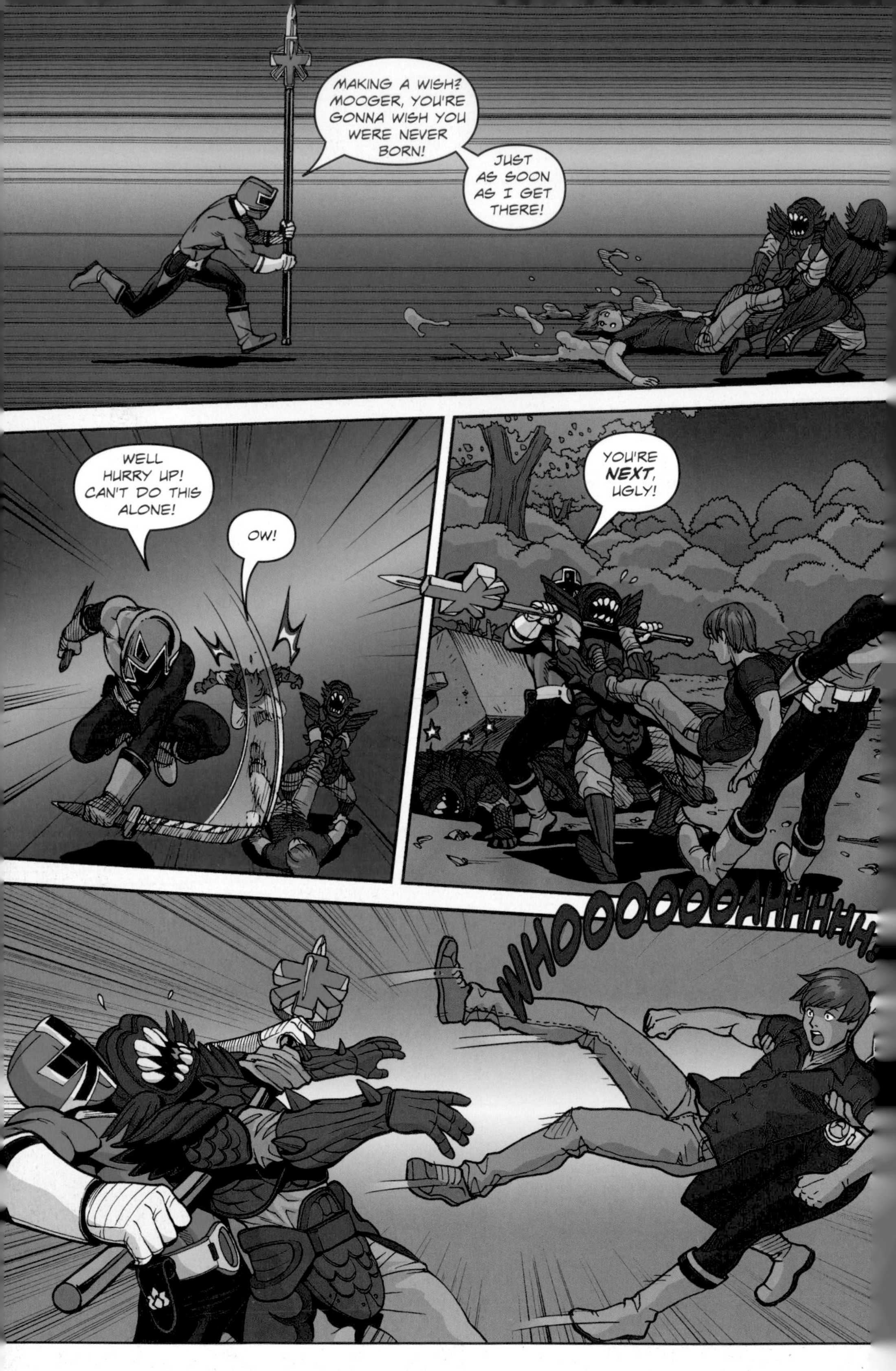
MAKING A WISH? MOOGER, YOU'RE GONNA WISH YOU WERE NEVER BORN!
JUST AS SOON AS I GET THERE!
WELL HURRY UP! CAN'T DO THIS ALONE!
OW!
YOU'RE NEXT, UGLY!
WHOOOOOOAHHHHH!

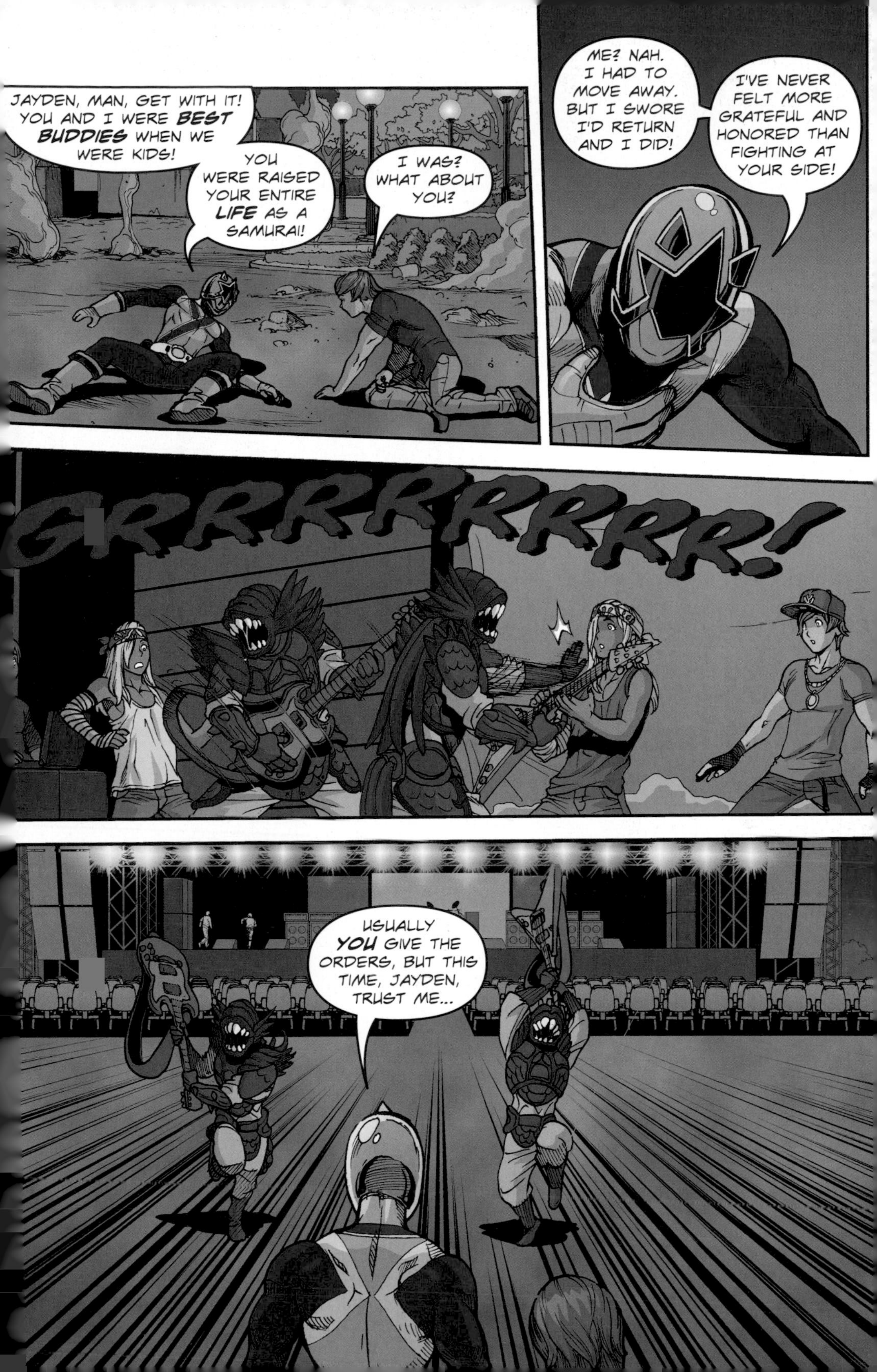
JAYDEN, MAN, GET WITH IT! YOU AND I WERE BEST BUDDIES WHEN WE WERE KIDS!
YOU WERE RAISED YOUR ENTIRE LIFE AS A SAMURAI!
I WAS? WHAT ABOUT YOU?
ME? NAH. I HAD TO MOVE AWAY. BUT I SWORE I'D RETURN AND I DID!
I'VE NEVER FELT MORE GRATEFUL AND HONORED THAN FIGHTING AT YOUR SIDE!
GRRRRRRRRR!
USUALLY YOU GIVE THE ORDERS, BUT THIS TIME, JAYDEN, TRUST ME...

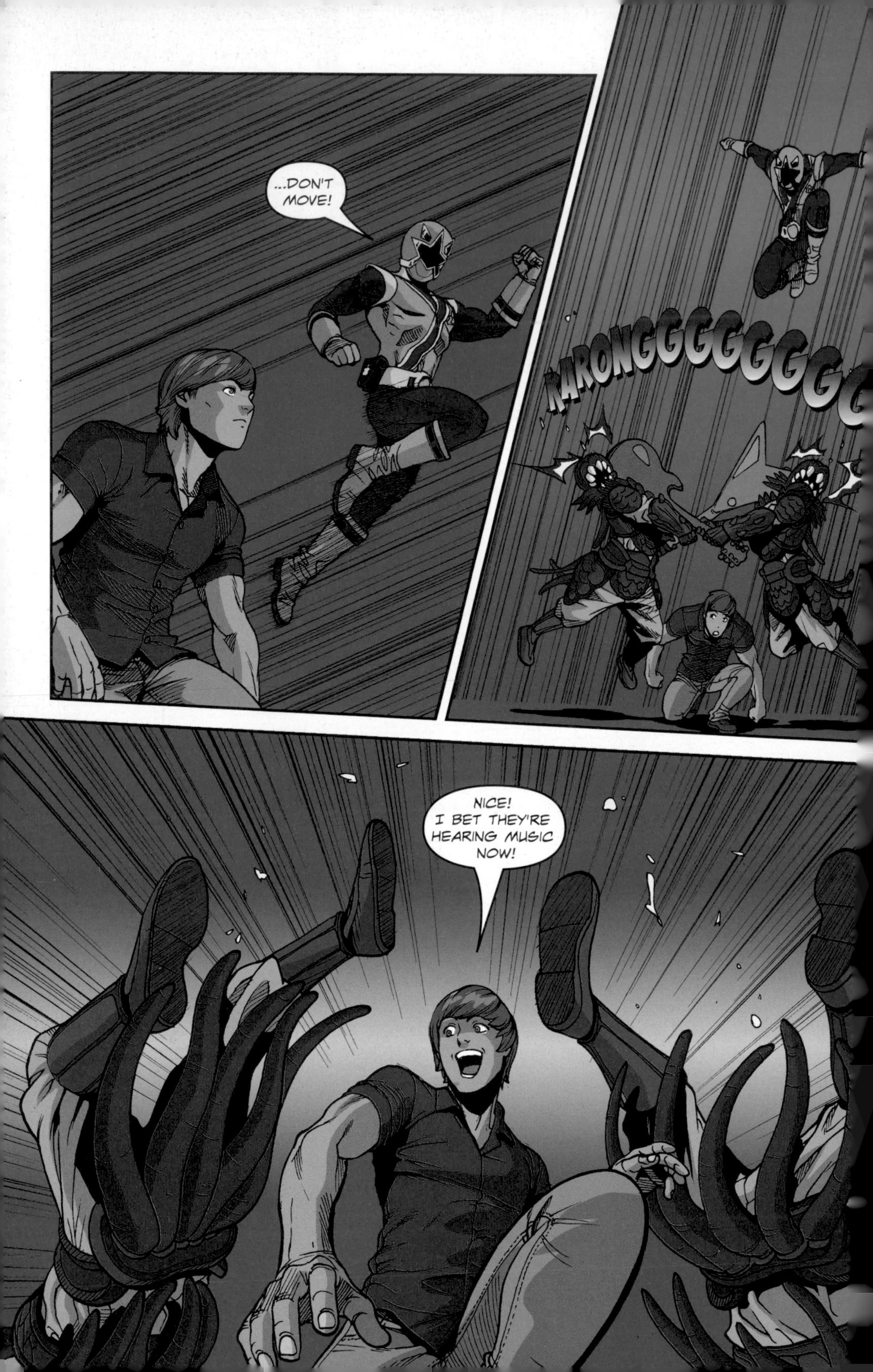
...DON'T MOVE!
KARONGGGGGGGGG
NICE! I BET THEY'RE HEARING MUSIC NOW!

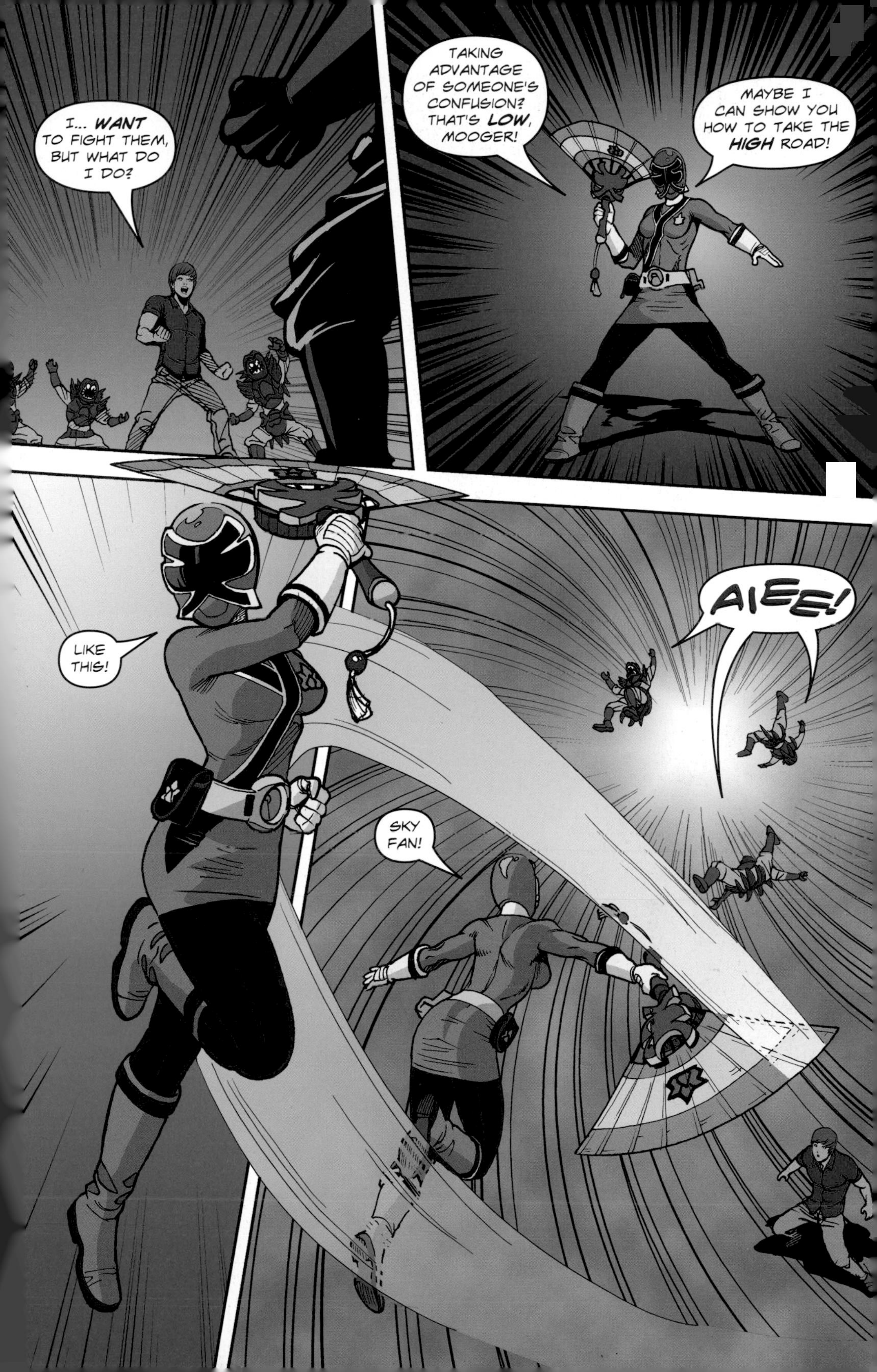
I... WANT TO FIGHT THEM, BUT WHAT DO I DO?
TAKING ADVANTAGE OF SOMEONE'S CONFUSION? THAT'S LOW, MOOGER!
MAYBE I CAN SHOW YOU HOW TO TAKE THE HIGH ROAD!
AIEE!
LIKE THIS!
SKY FAN!

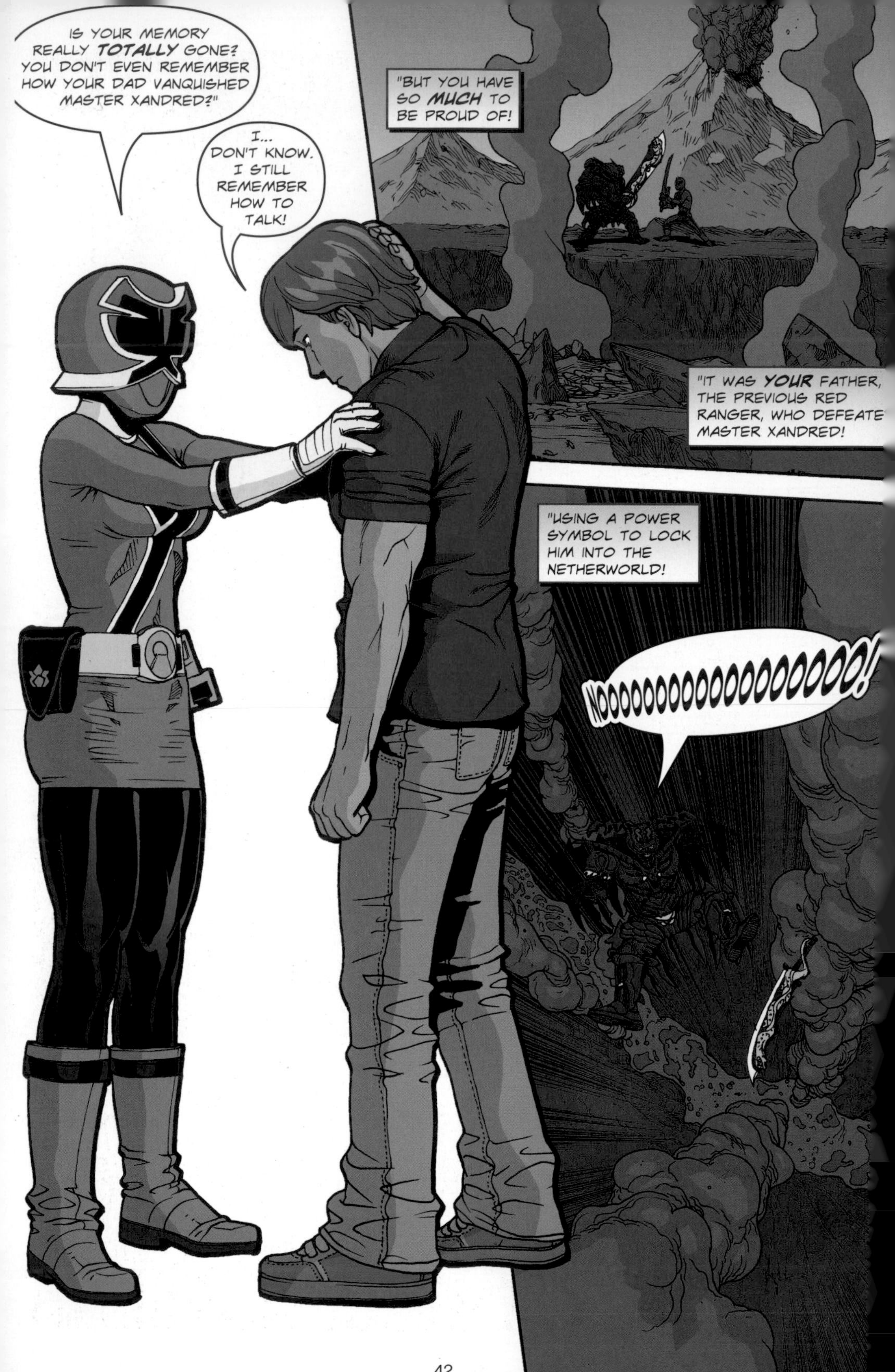
IS YOUR MEMORY REALLY TOTALLY GONE? YOU DON'T EVEN REMEMBER HOW YOUR DAD VANQUISHED MASTER XANDRED?"
I... DON'T KNOW. I STILL REMEMBER HOW TO TALK!
"BUT YOU HAVE SO MUCH TO BE PROUD OF!
"IT WAS YOUR FATHER, THE PREVIOUS RED RANGER, WHO DEFEATE MASTER XANDRED!
"USING A POWER SYMBOL TO LOCK HIM INTO THE NETHERWORLD!
NOOOOOOOOOOOOOOOOOO!

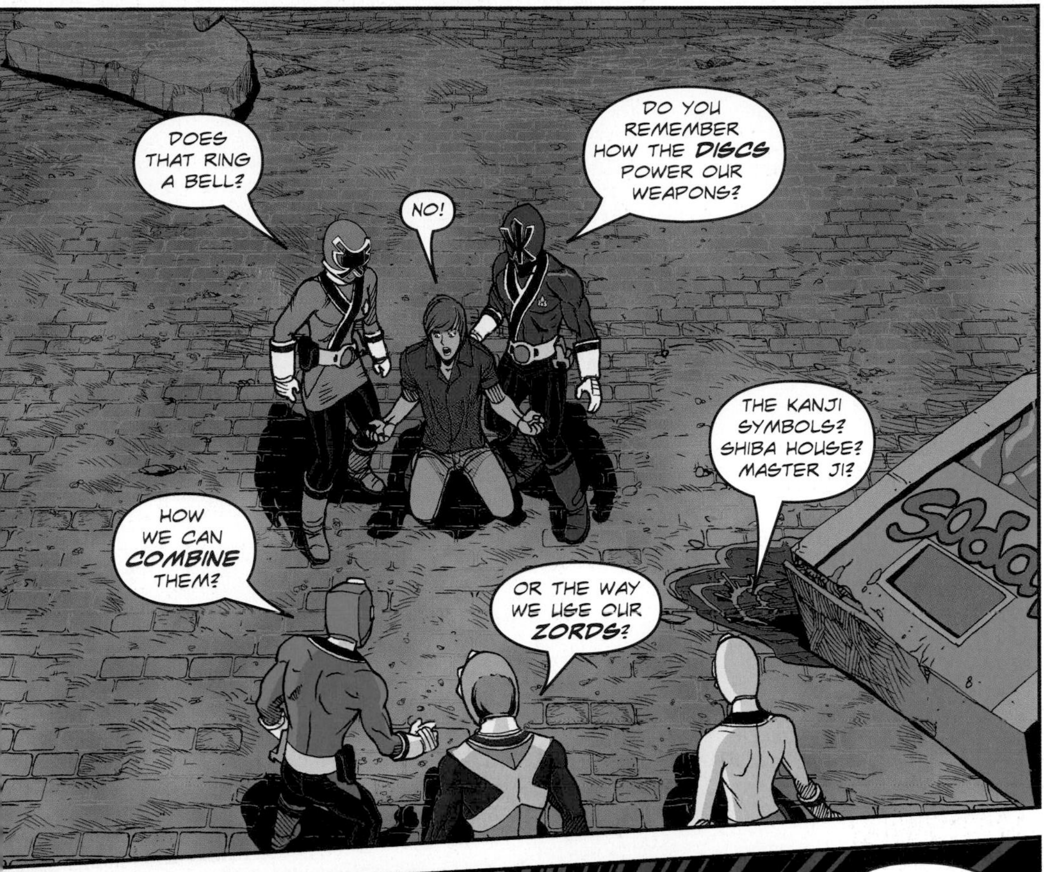
DOES THAT RING A BELL?
DO YOU REMEMBER HOW THE DISCS POWER OUR WEAPONS?
NO!
THE KANJI SYMBOLS? SHIBA HOUSE? MASTER JI!?
HOW WE CAN COMBINE THEM?
OR THE WAY WE USE OUR ZORDS?

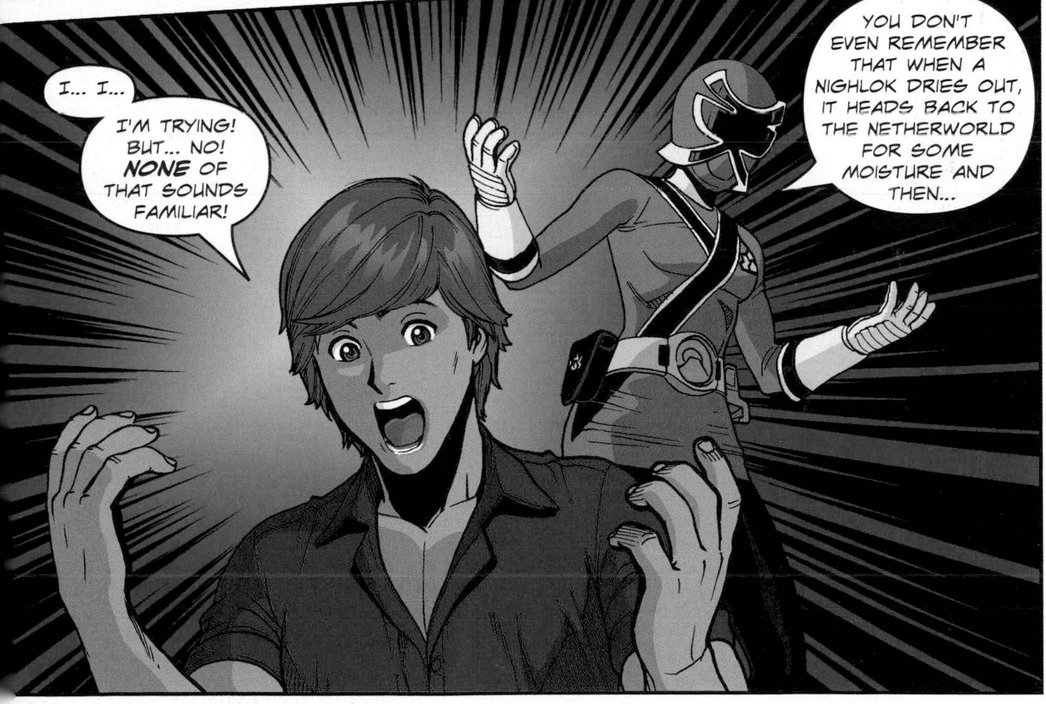
I... I...
I'M TRYING! BUT... NO! NONE OF THAT SOUNDS FAMILIAR!
YOU DON'T EVEN REMEMBER THAT WHEN A NIGHLOK DRIES OUT, IT HEADS BACK TO THE NETHERWORLD FOR SOME MOISTURE AND THEN...

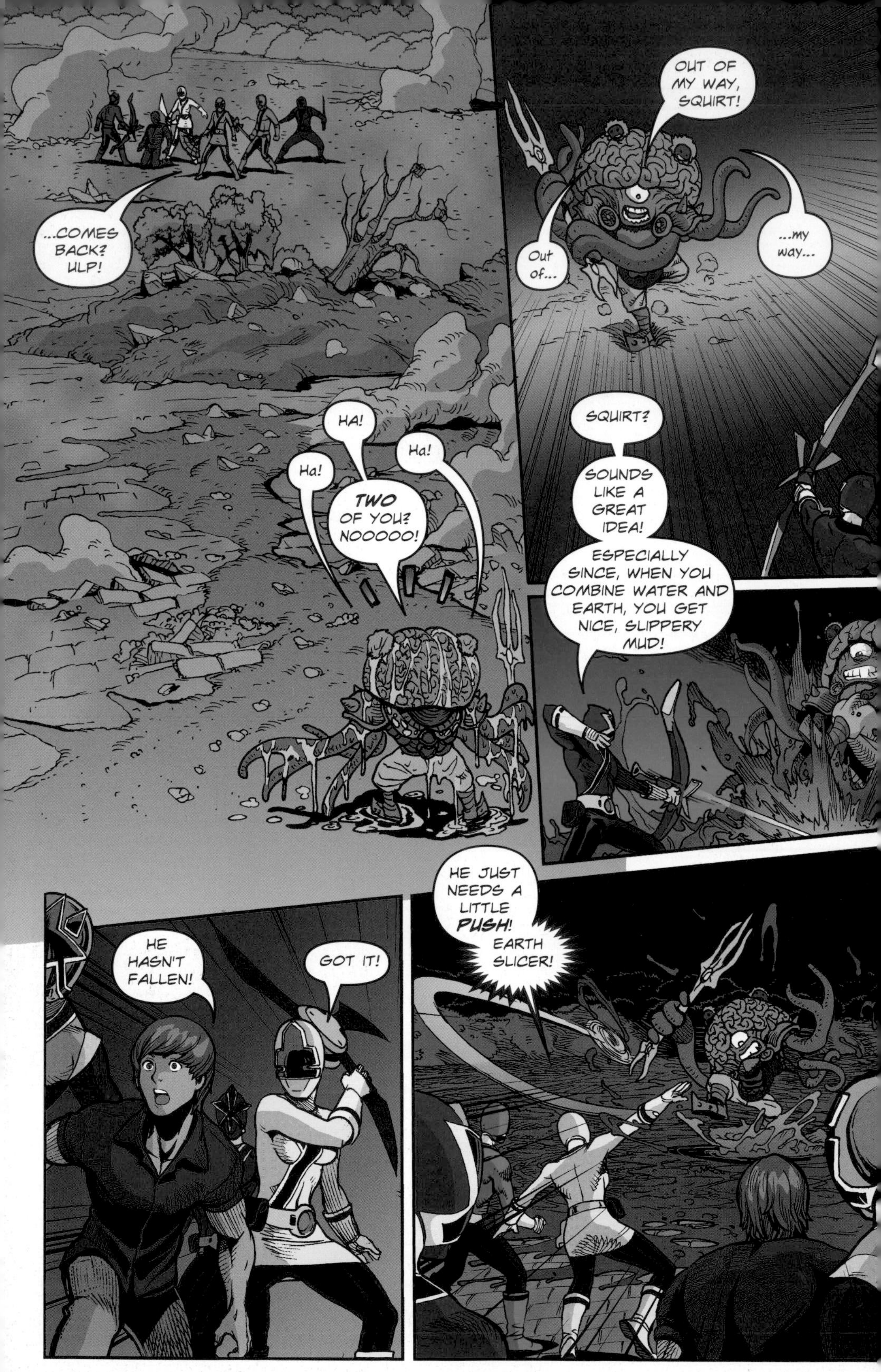
...COMES BACK? ULP!
OUT OF MY WAY, SQUIRT!
Out of...
...my way...
HA!
Ha!
Ha!
TWO OF YOU? NOOOOO!
SQUIRT?
SOUNDS LIKE A GREAT IDEA!
ESPECIALLY SINCE, WHEN YOU COMBINE WATER AND EARTH, YOU GET NICE, SLIPPERY MUD!
HE HASN'T FALLEN!
GOT IT!
HE JUST NEEDS A LITTLE PUSH!
EARTH SLICER!

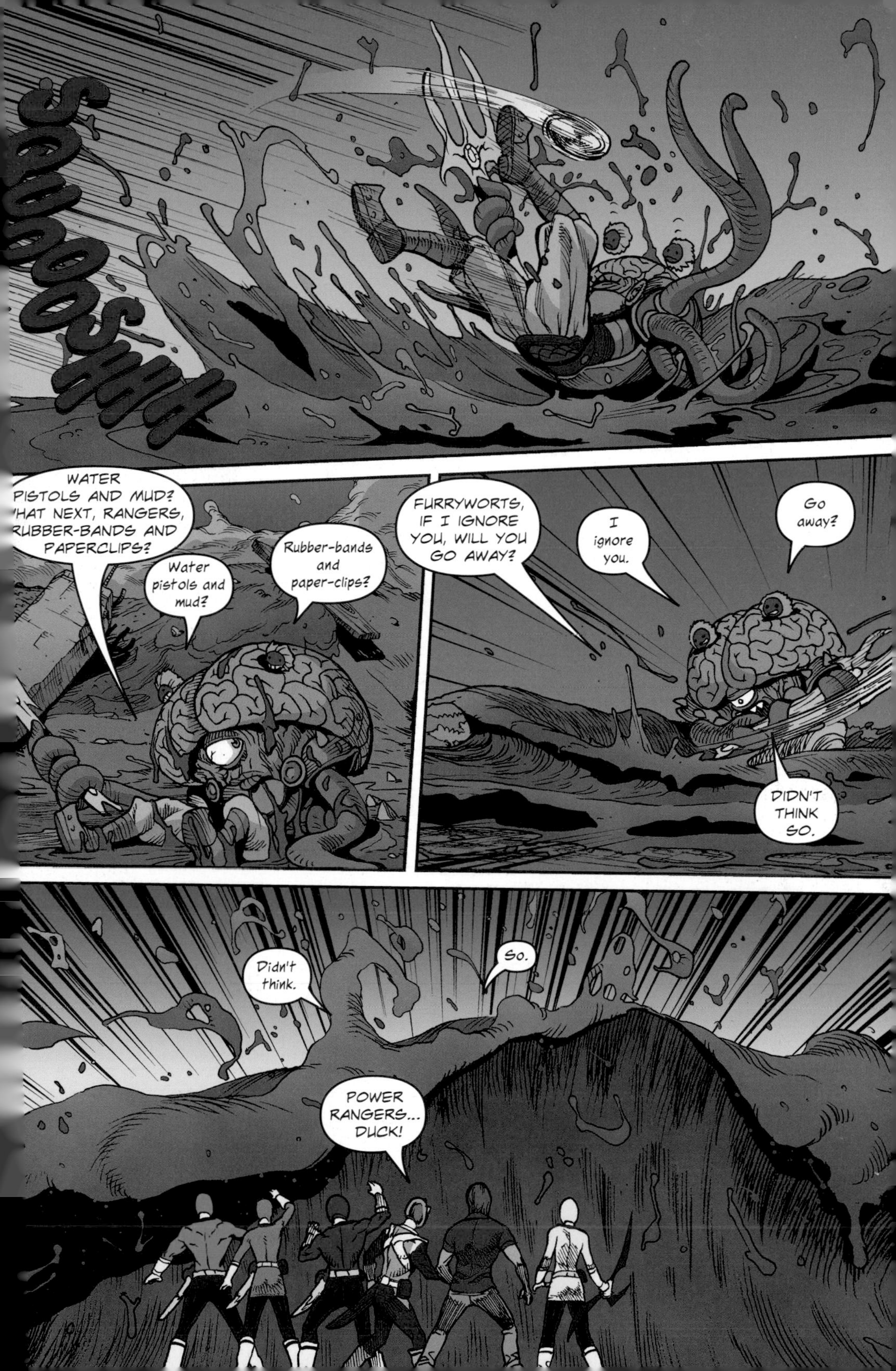
SQUOOOOSHHH
WATER PISTOLS AND MUD? WHAT NEXT, RANGERS, RUBBER-BANDS AND PAPERCLIPS?
Water pistols and mud?
Rubber-bands and paper-clips?
FURRYWORTS, IF I IGNORE YOU, WILL YOU GO AWAY?
I ignore you.
Go away?
DIDN'T THINK SO.
Didn't think.
So.
POWER RANGERS... DUCK!

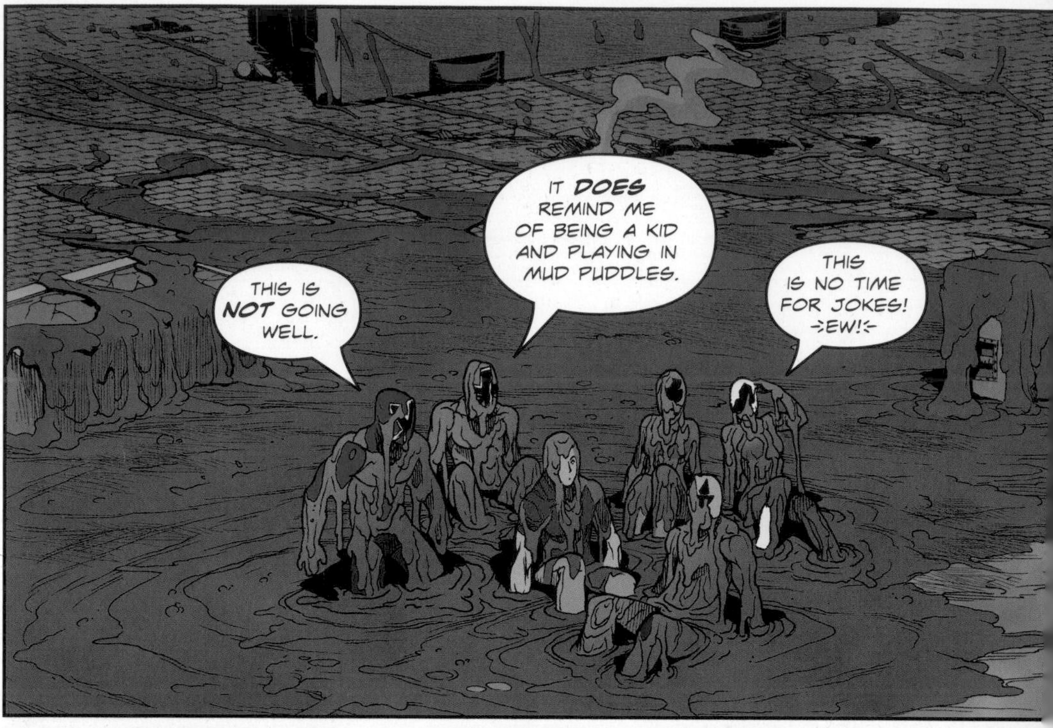
THIS IS NOT GOING WELL.
IT DOES REMIND ME OF BEING A KID AND PLAYING IN MUD PUDDLES.
THIS IS NO TIME FOR JOKES! EW!

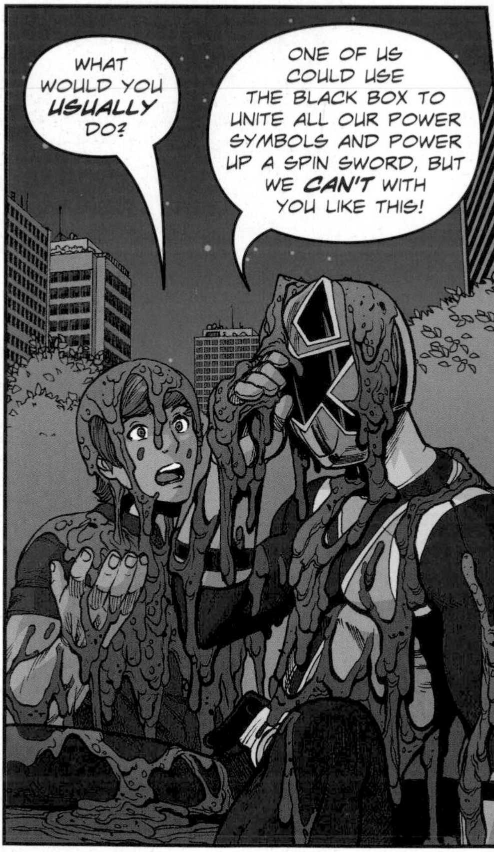
WHAT WOULD YOU USUALLY DO?
ONE OF US COULD USE THE BLACK BOX TO UNITE ALL OUR POWER SYMBOLS AND POWER UP A SPIN SWORD, BUT WE CAN'T WITH YOU LIKE THIS!

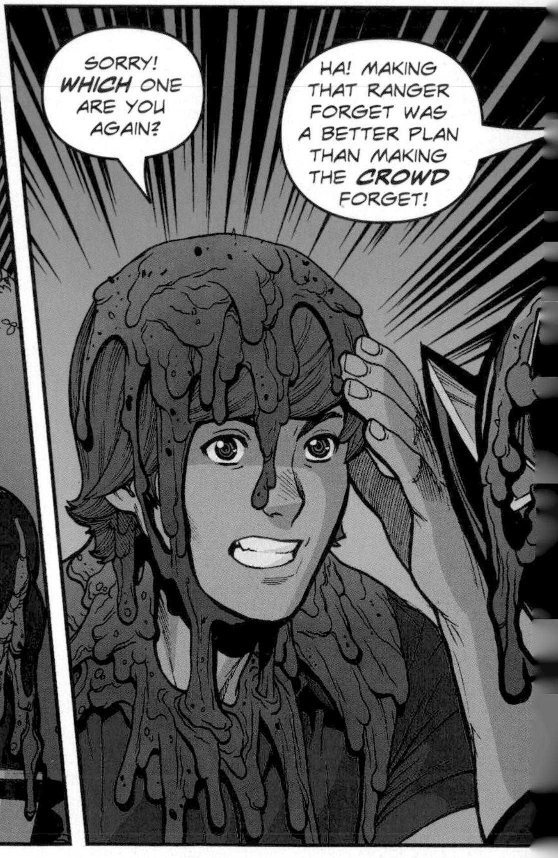
SORRY! WHICH ONE ARE YOU AGAIN?
HA! MAKING THAT RANGER FORGET WAS A BETTER PLAN THAN MAKING THE CROWD FORGET!

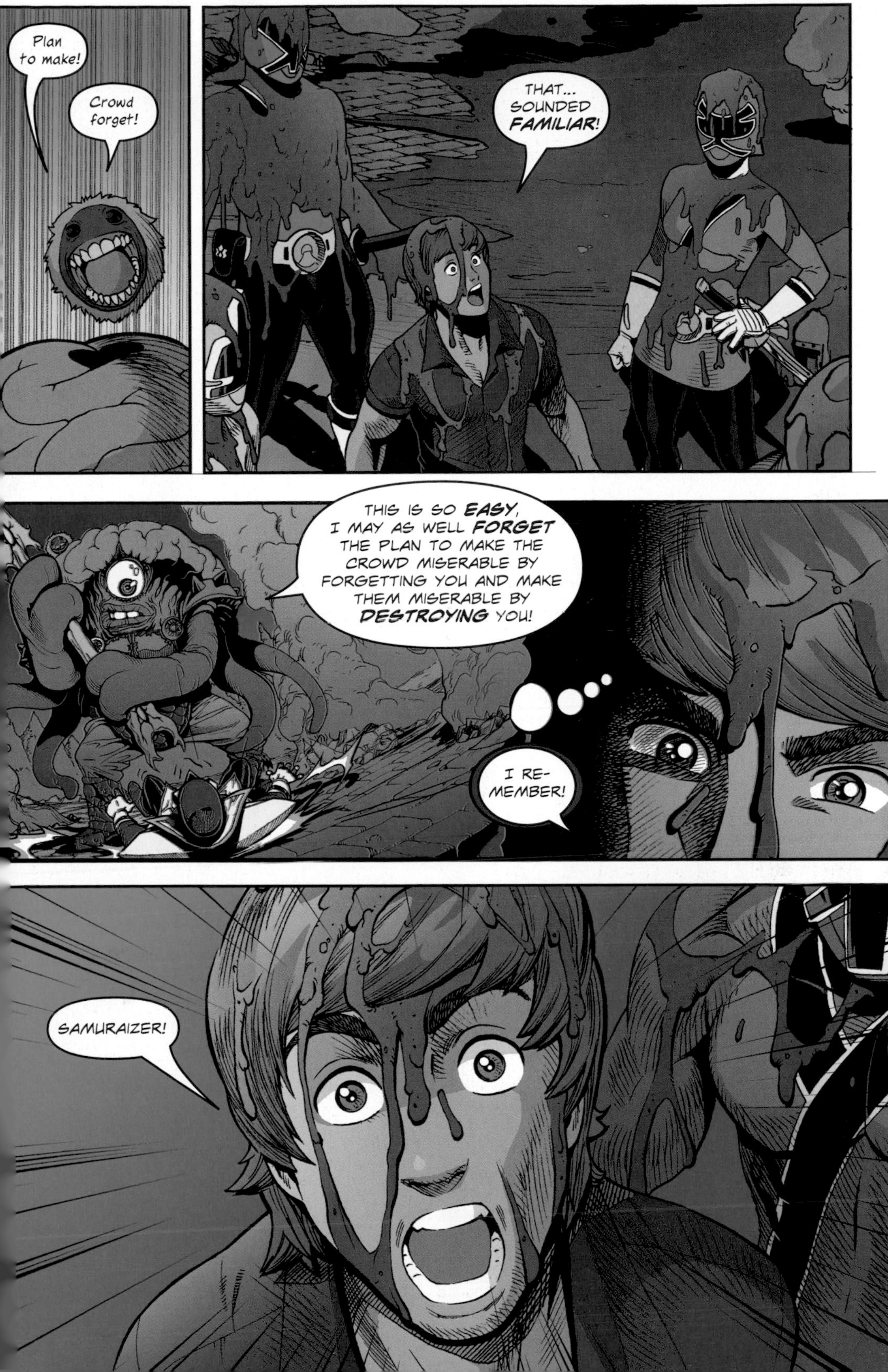
Plan to make!
Crowd forget!
THAT... SOUNDED FAMILIAR!
THIS IS SO EASY, I MAY AS WELL FORGET THE PLAN TO MAKE THE CROWD MISERABLE BY FORGETTING YOU AND MAKE THEM MISERABLE BY DESTROYING YOU!
I RE-MEMBER!
SAMURAIZER!

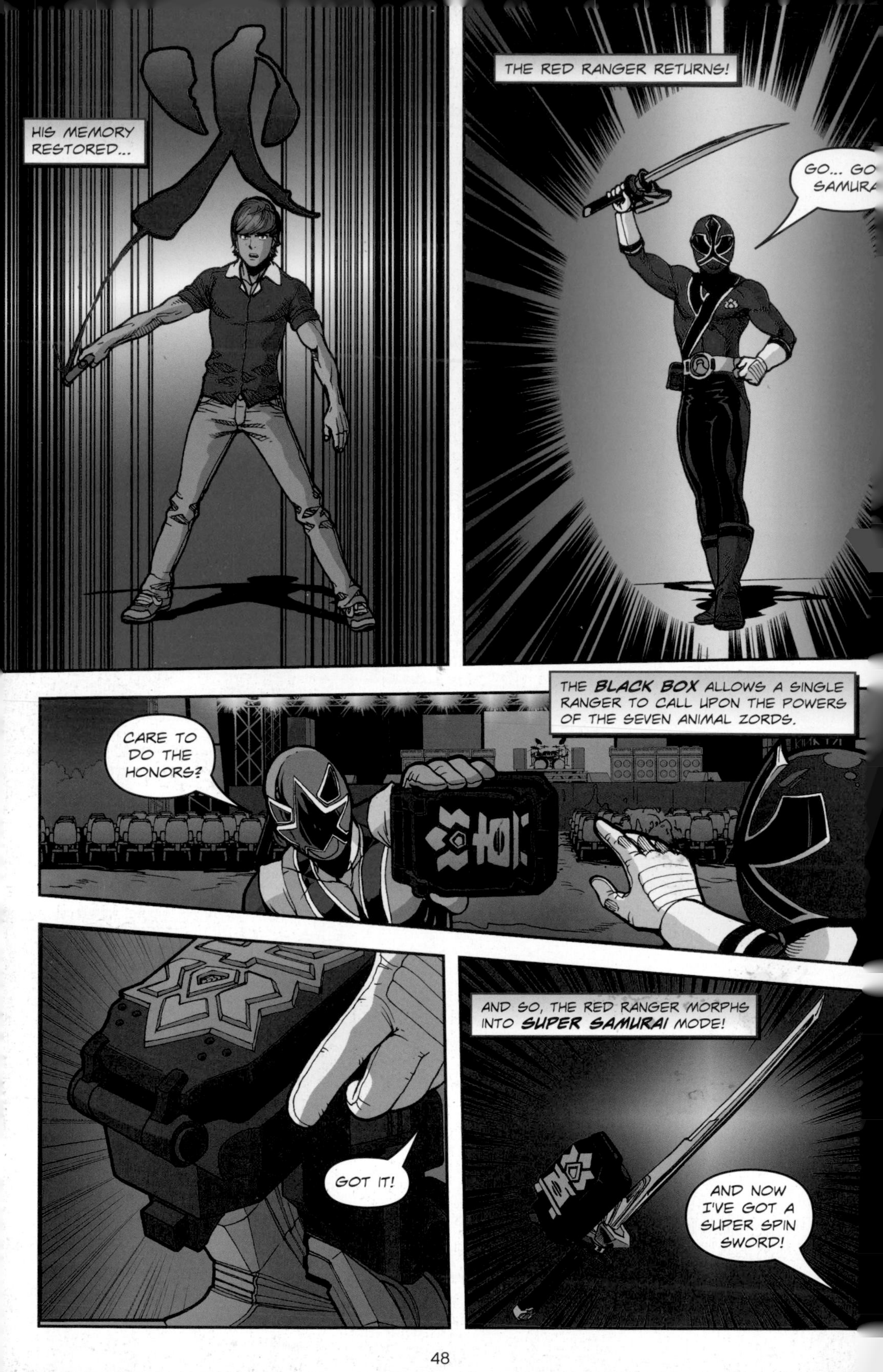
HIS MEMORY RESTORED...
THE RED RANGER RETURNS!
GO... GO SAMURA
THE BLACK BOX ALLOWS A SINGLE RANGER TO CALL UPON THE POWERS OF THE SEVEN ANIMAL ZORDS.
CARE TO DO THE HONORS?
GOT IT!
AND SO, THE RED RANGER MORPHS INTO SUPER SAMURAI MODE!
AND NOW I'VE GOT A SUPER SPIN SWORD!

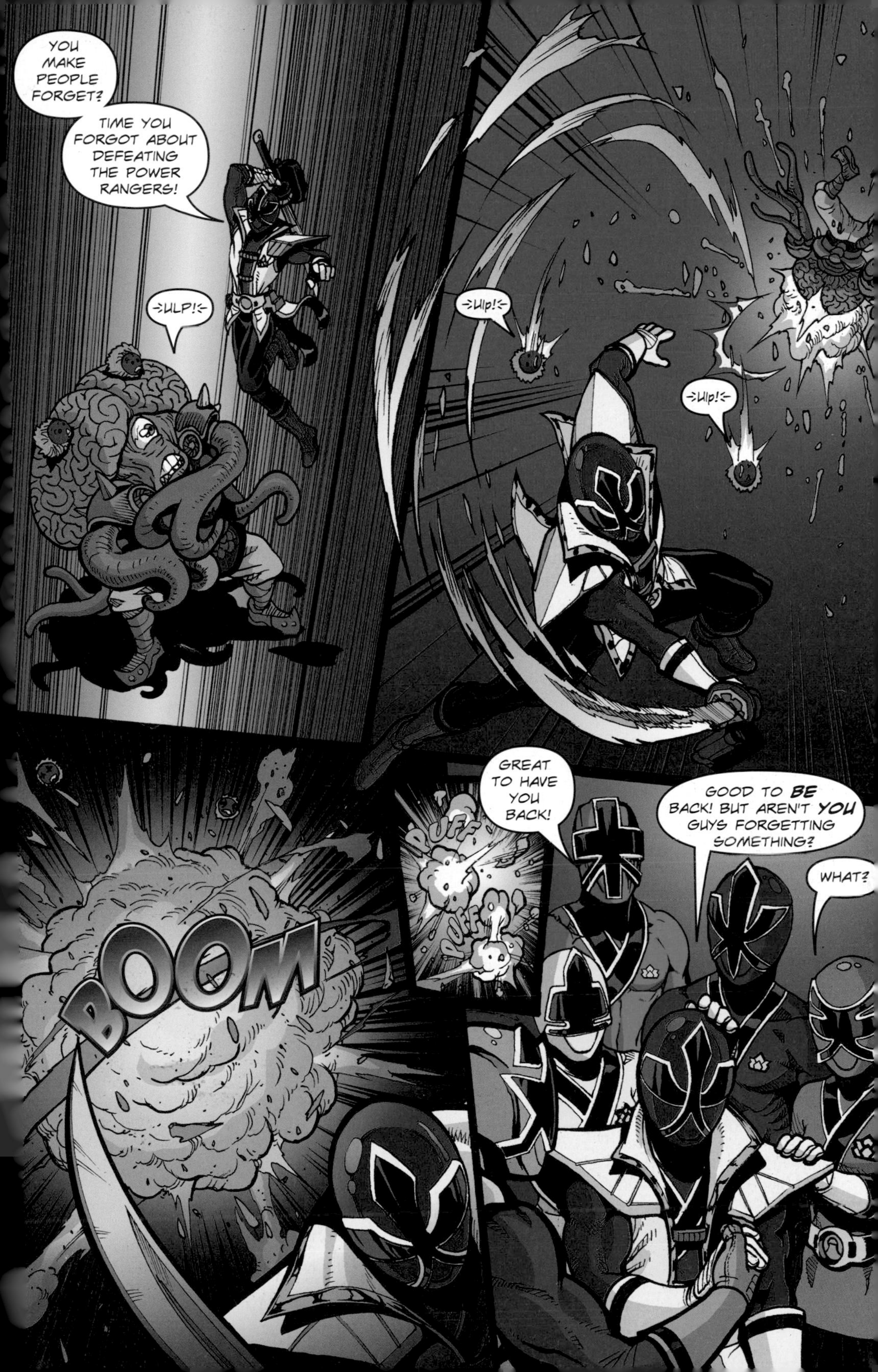

YOU MAKE PEOPLE FORGET?
TIME YOU FORGOT ABOUT DEFEATING THE POWER RANGERS!
-ULP!-
-Ulp!-
-Ulp!-
BOOM
GREAT TO HAVE YOU BACK!
PUFF
PUFF
GOOD TO **BE** BACK! BUT AREN'T ***YOU*** GUYS FORGETTING SOMETHING?
WHAT?

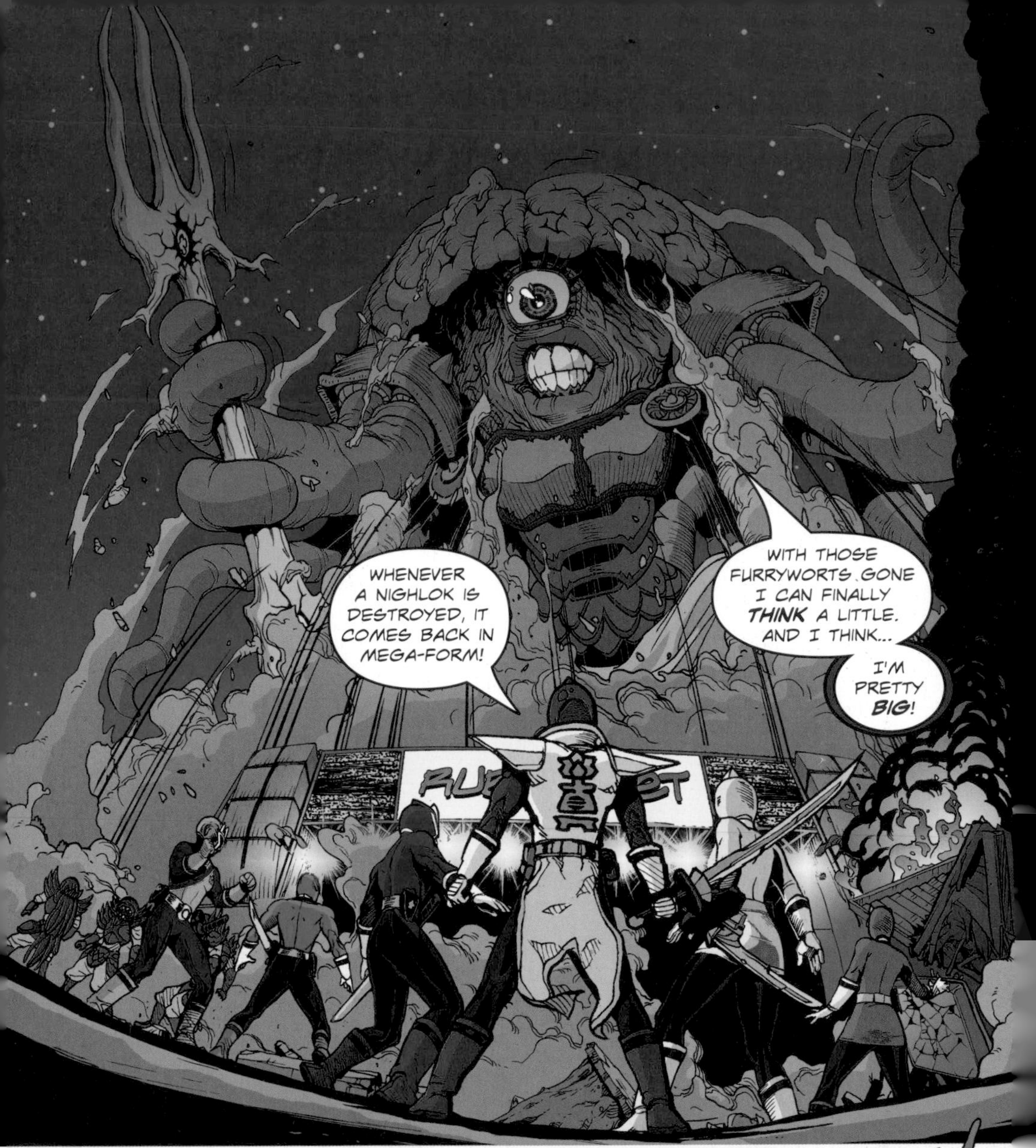
WHENEVER A NIGHLOK IS DESTROYED, IT COMES BACK IN MEGA-FORM!
WITH THOSE FURRYWORTS GONE I CAN FINALLY THINK A LITTLE. AND I THINK...
I'M PRETTY BIG!

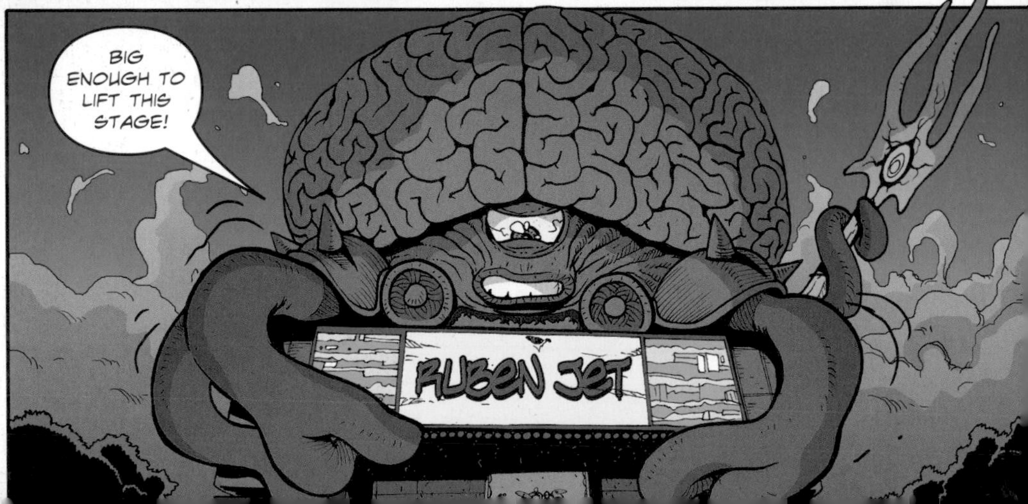
BIG ENOUGH TO LIFT THIS STAGE!
RUBEN JET

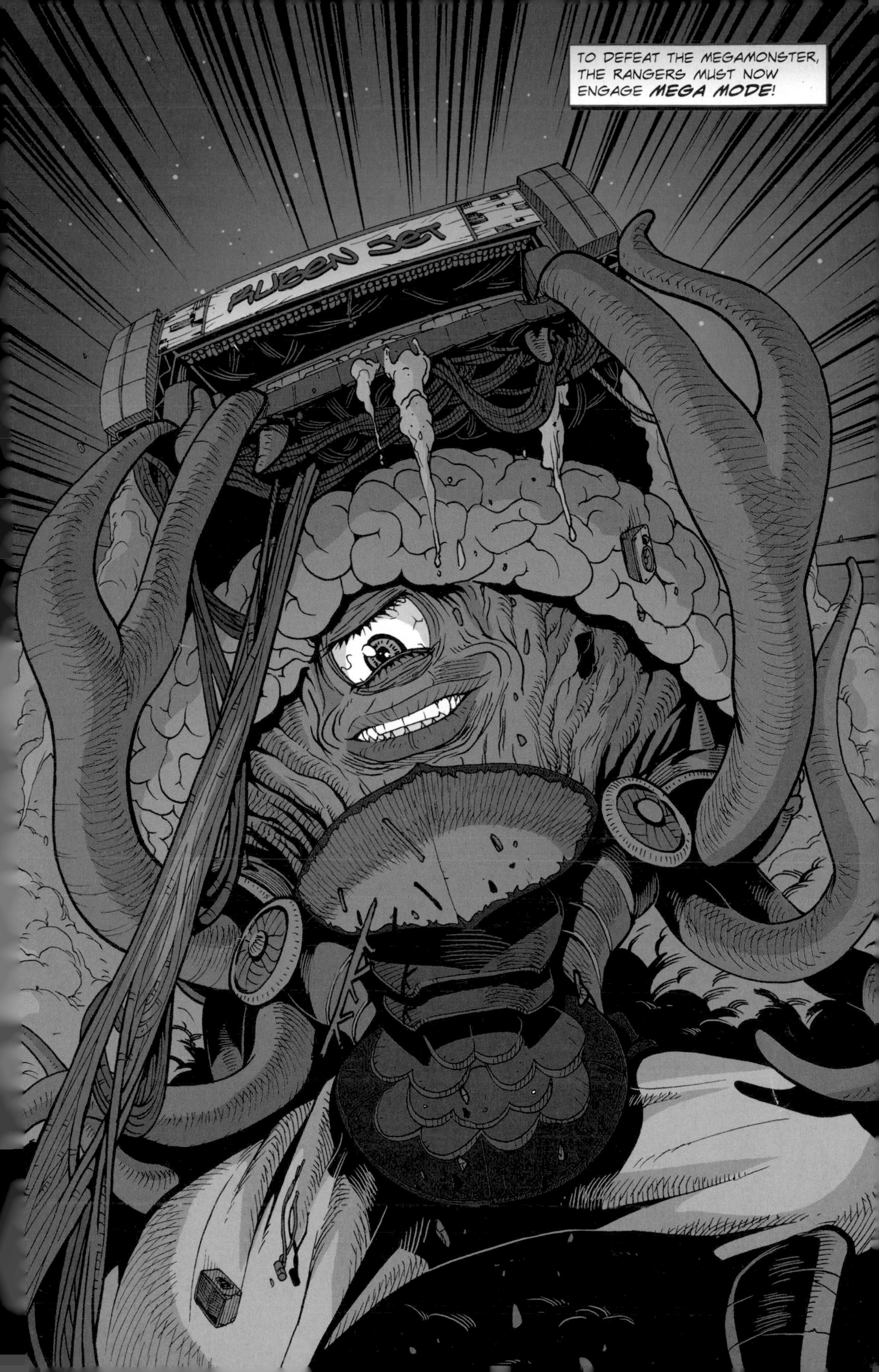
TO DEFEAT THE MEGAMONSTER, THE RANGERS MUST NOW ENGAGE MEGA MODE!
FLUBEN JET

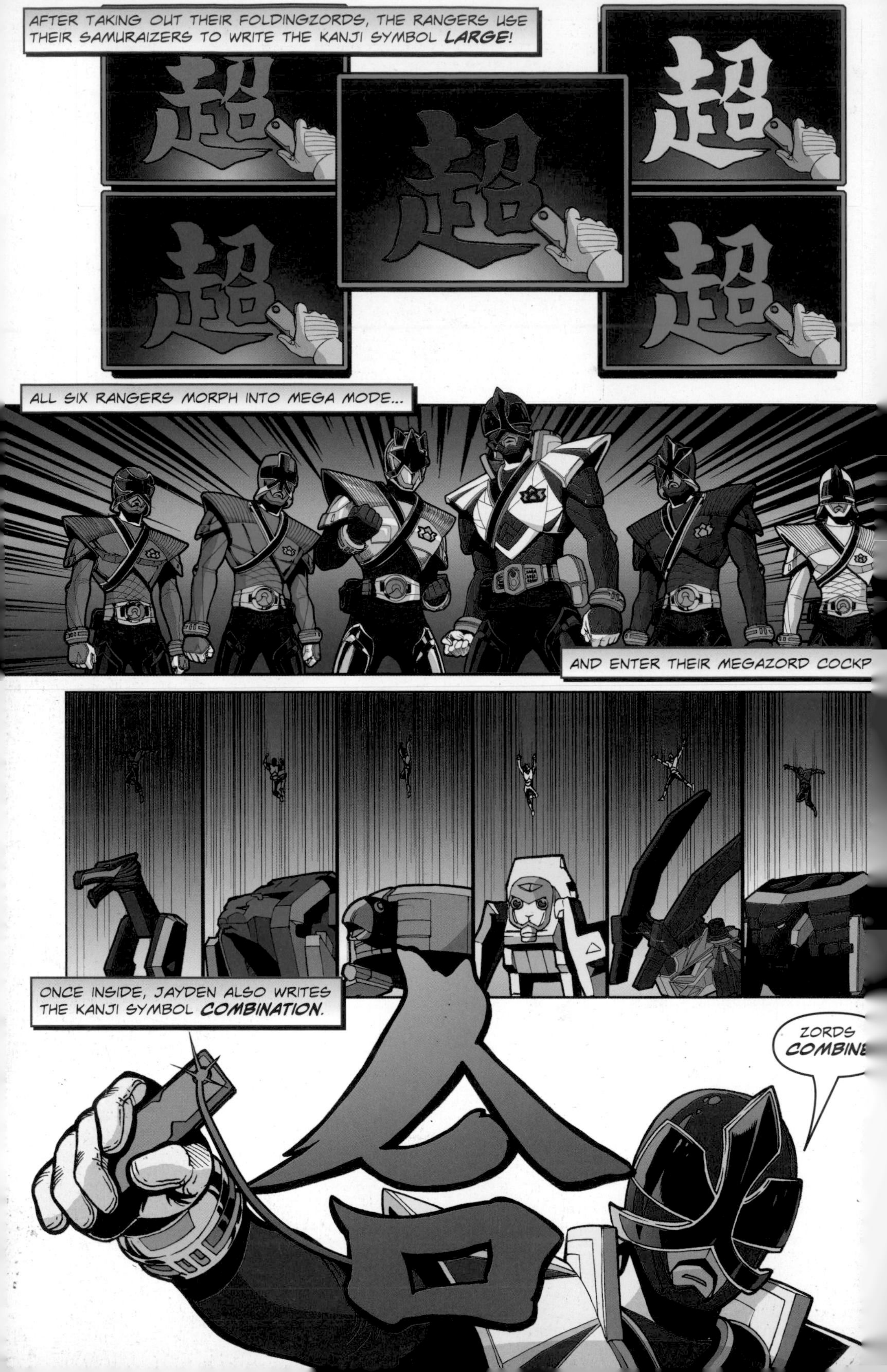
AFTER TAKING OUT THEIR FOLDINGZORDS, THE RANGERS USE THEIR SAMURAIZERS TO WRITE THE KANJI SYMBOL LARGE!
超
ALL SIX RANGERS MORPH INTO MEGA MODE...
AND ENTER THEIR MEGAZORD COCKP
ONCE INSIDE, JAYDEN ALSO WRITES THE KANJI SYMBOL COMBINATION.
ZORDS COMBINE

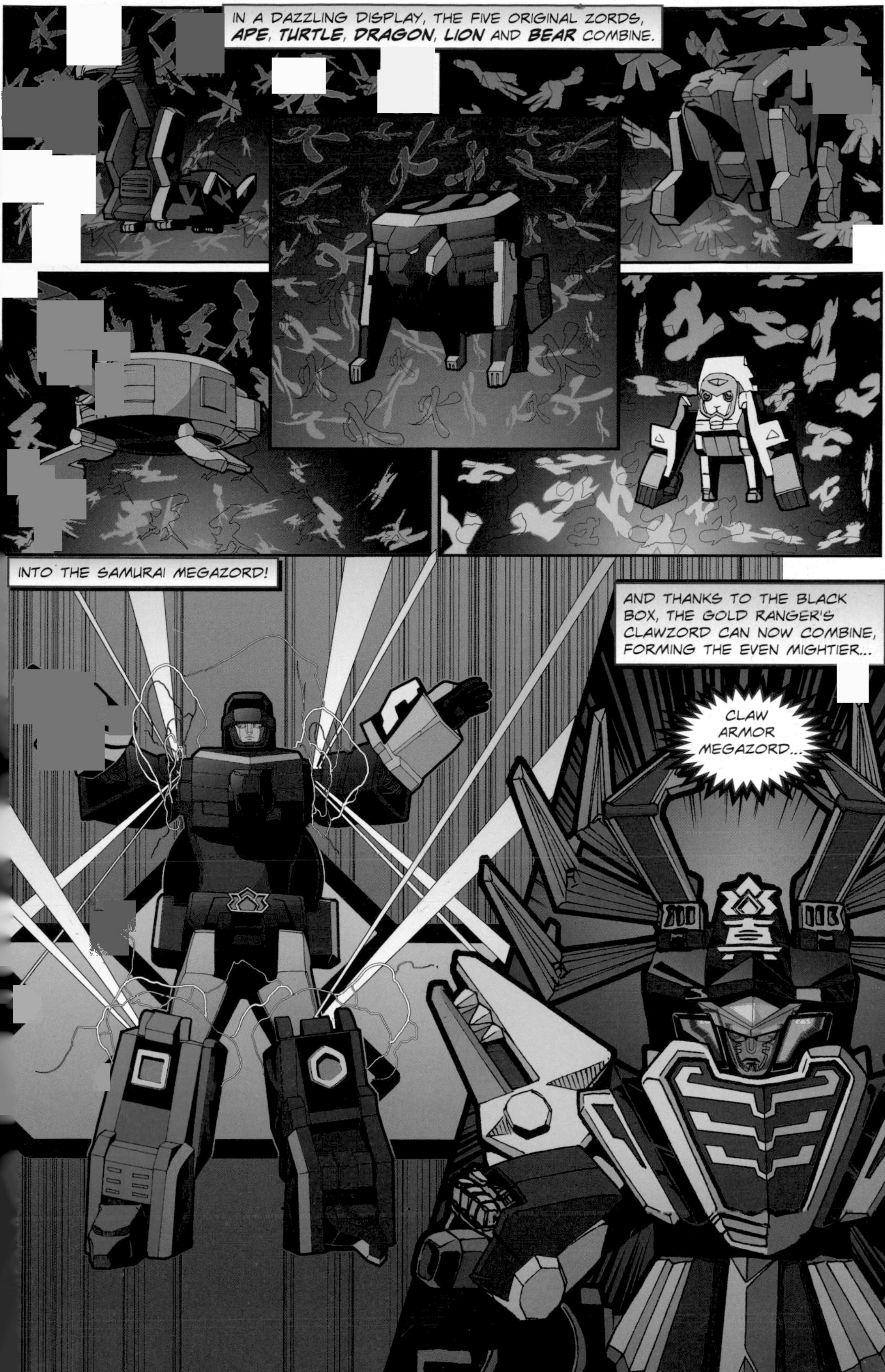
IN A DAZZLING DISPLAY, THE FIVE ORIGINAL ZORDS, APE, TURTLE, DRAGON, LION AND BEAR COMBINE.
INTO THE SAMURAI MEGAZORD!
AND THANKS TO THE BLACK BOX, THE GOLD RANGER'S CLAWZORD CAN NOW COMBINE, FORMING THE EVEN MIGHTIER...
CLAW ARMOR MEGAZORD...

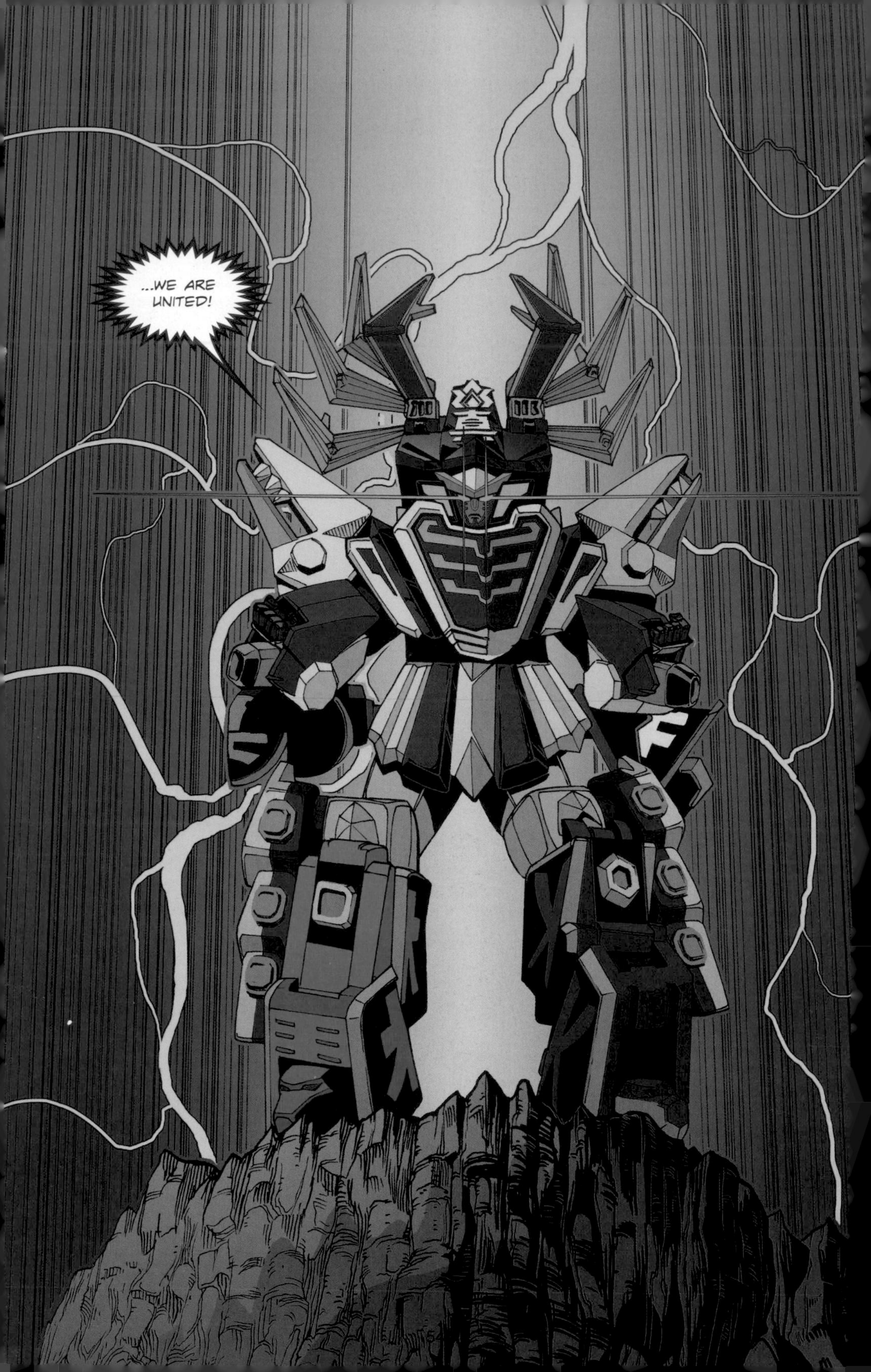
...WE ARE UNITED!

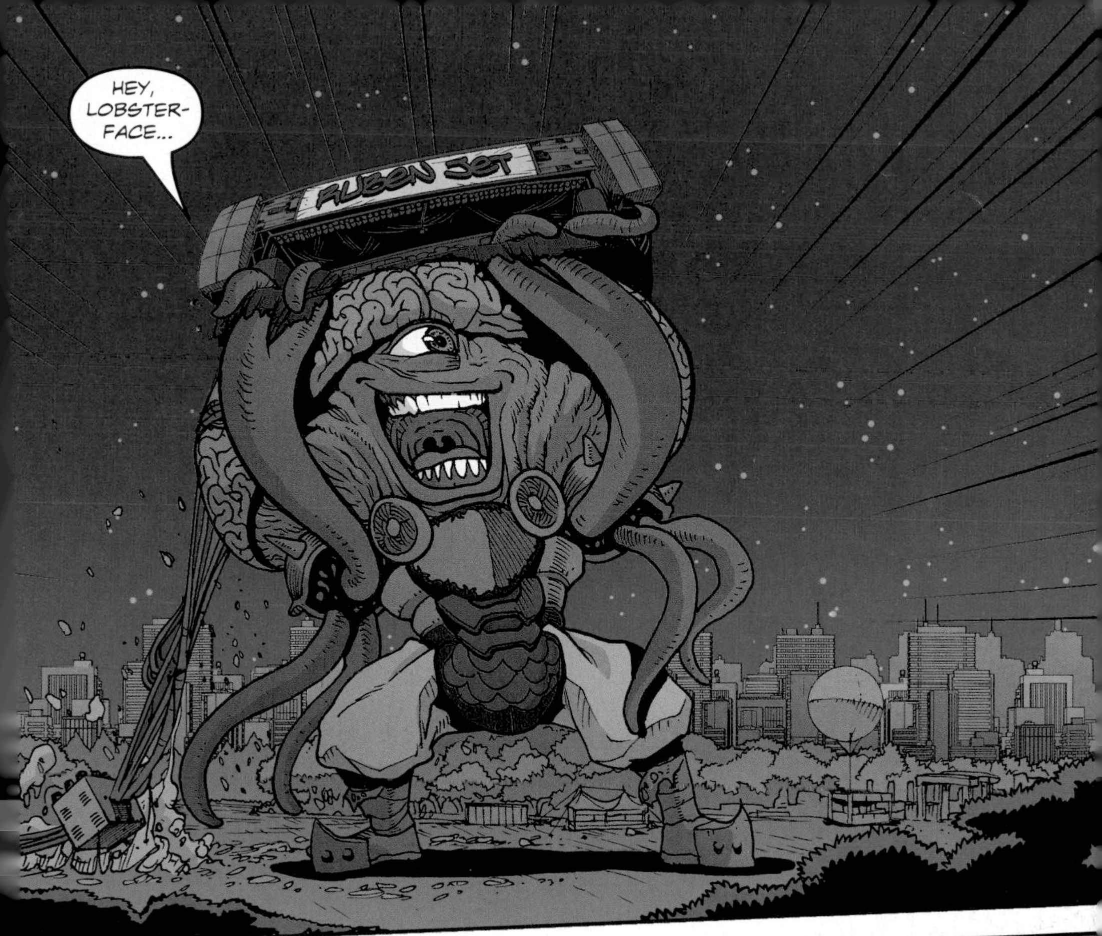
HEY, LOBSTER-FACE...
RUBEN JET

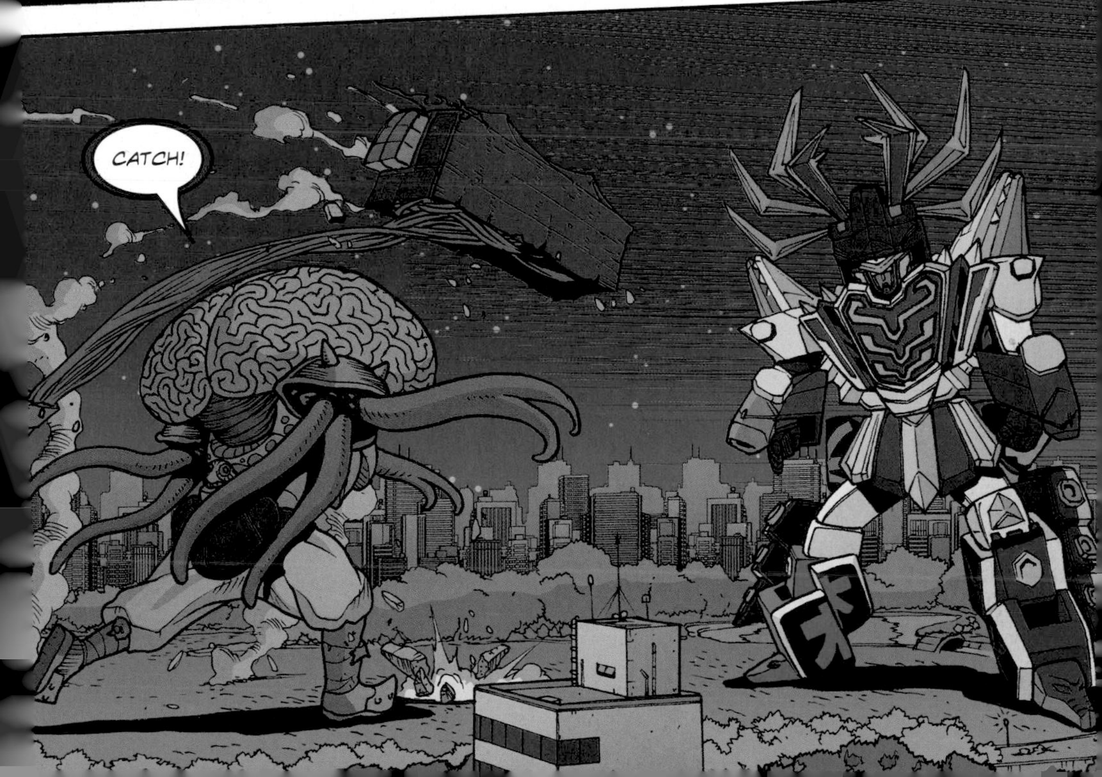
CATCH!

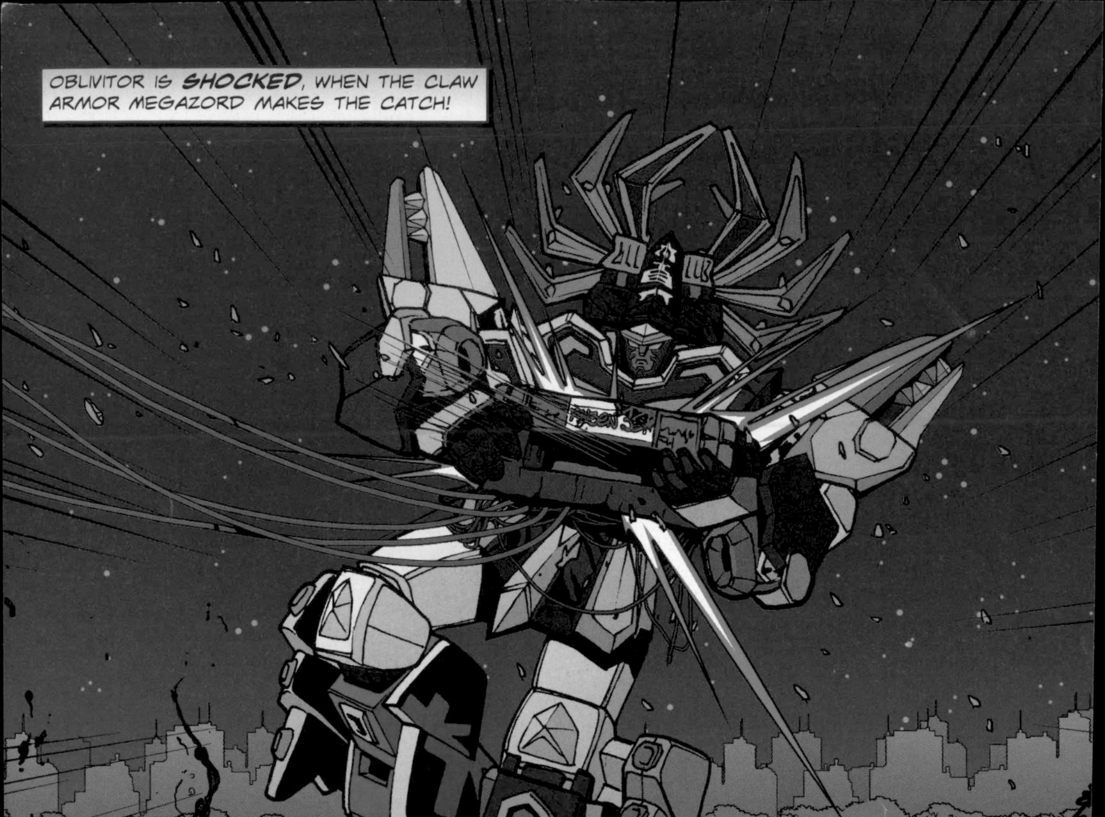
OBLIVITOR IS SHOCKED, WHEN THE CLAW ARMOR MEGAZORD MAKES THE CATCH!

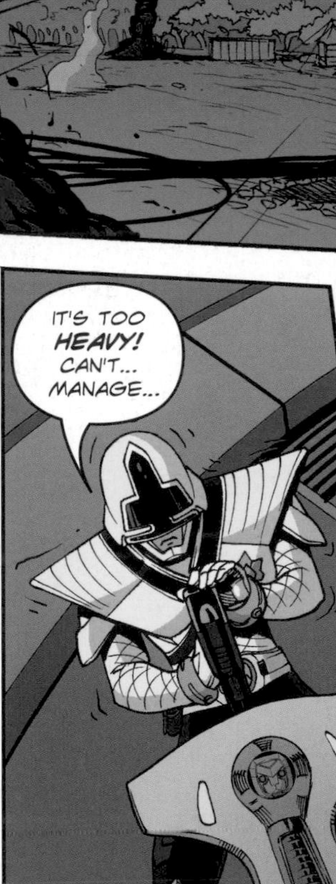
IT'S TOO HEAVY! CAN'T... MANAGE...

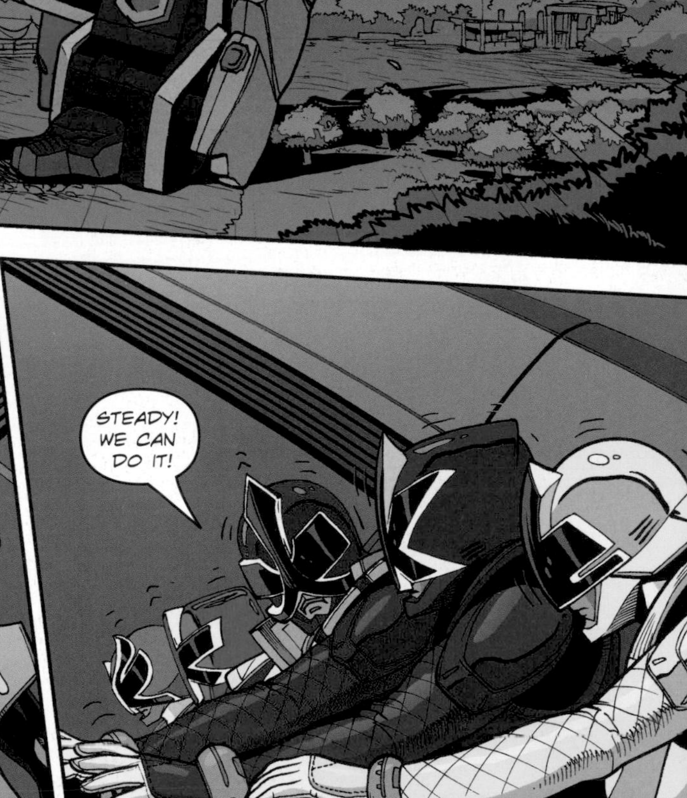
STEADY! WE CAN DO IT!

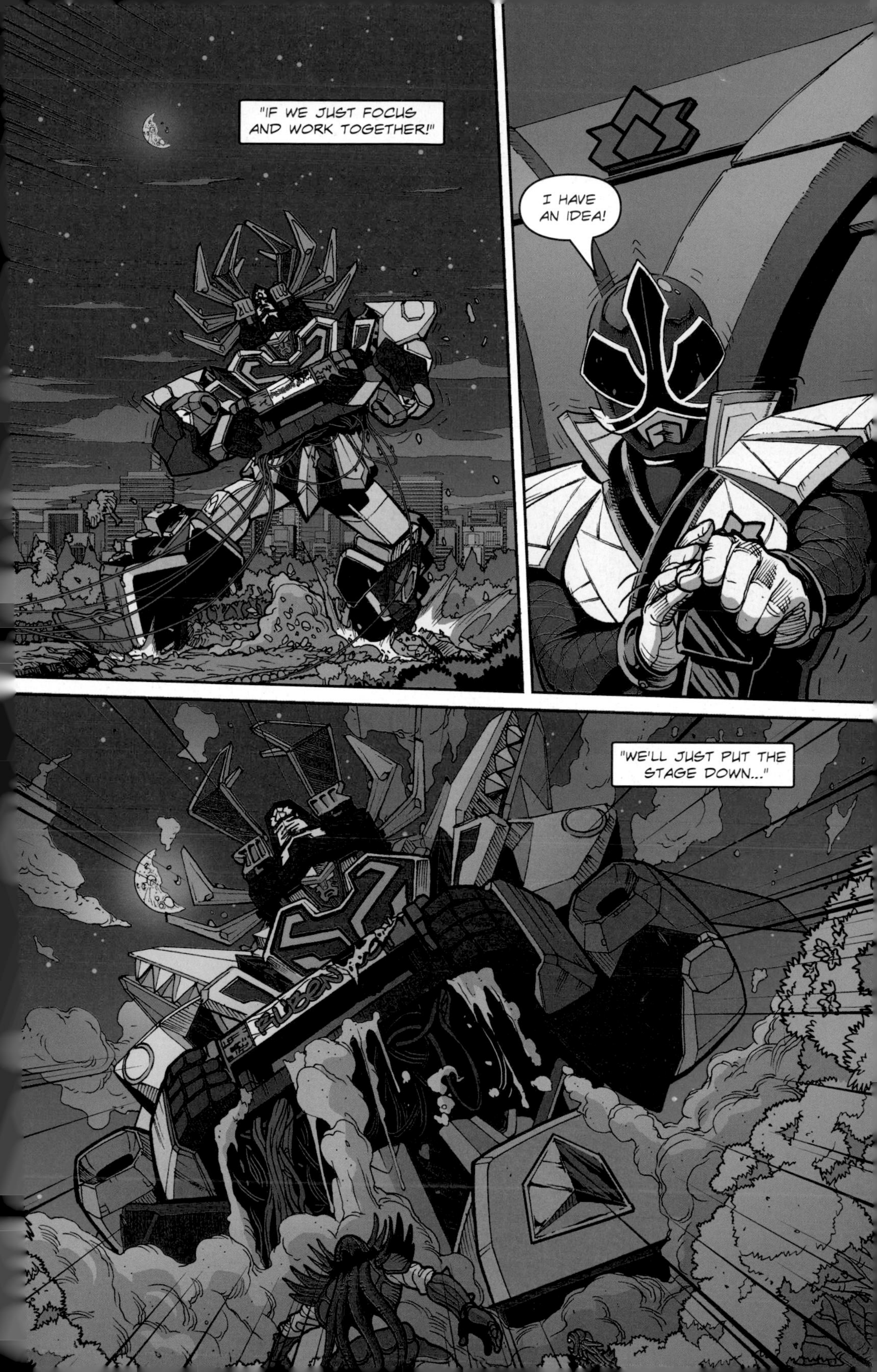
"IF WE JUST FOCUS AND WORK TOGETHER!"
I HAVE AN IDEA!
"WE'LL JUST PUT THE STAGE DOWN..."

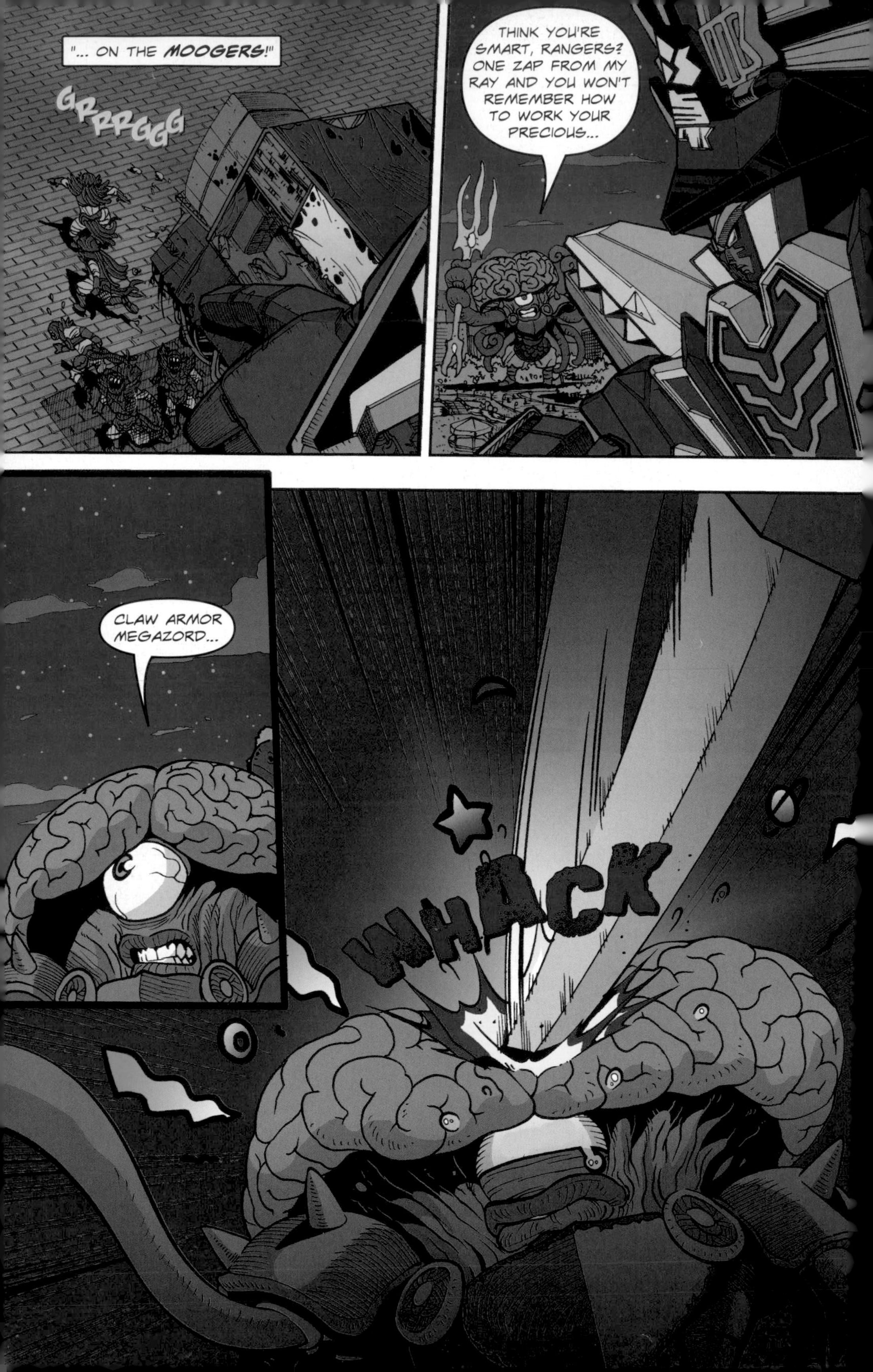
"... ON THE MOOGERS!"
GRRRGGG
THINK YOU'RE SMART, RANGERS? ONE ZAP FROM MY RAY AND YOU WON'T REMEMBER HOW TO WORK YOUR PRECIOUS...
CLAW ARMOR MEGAZORD...
WHACK

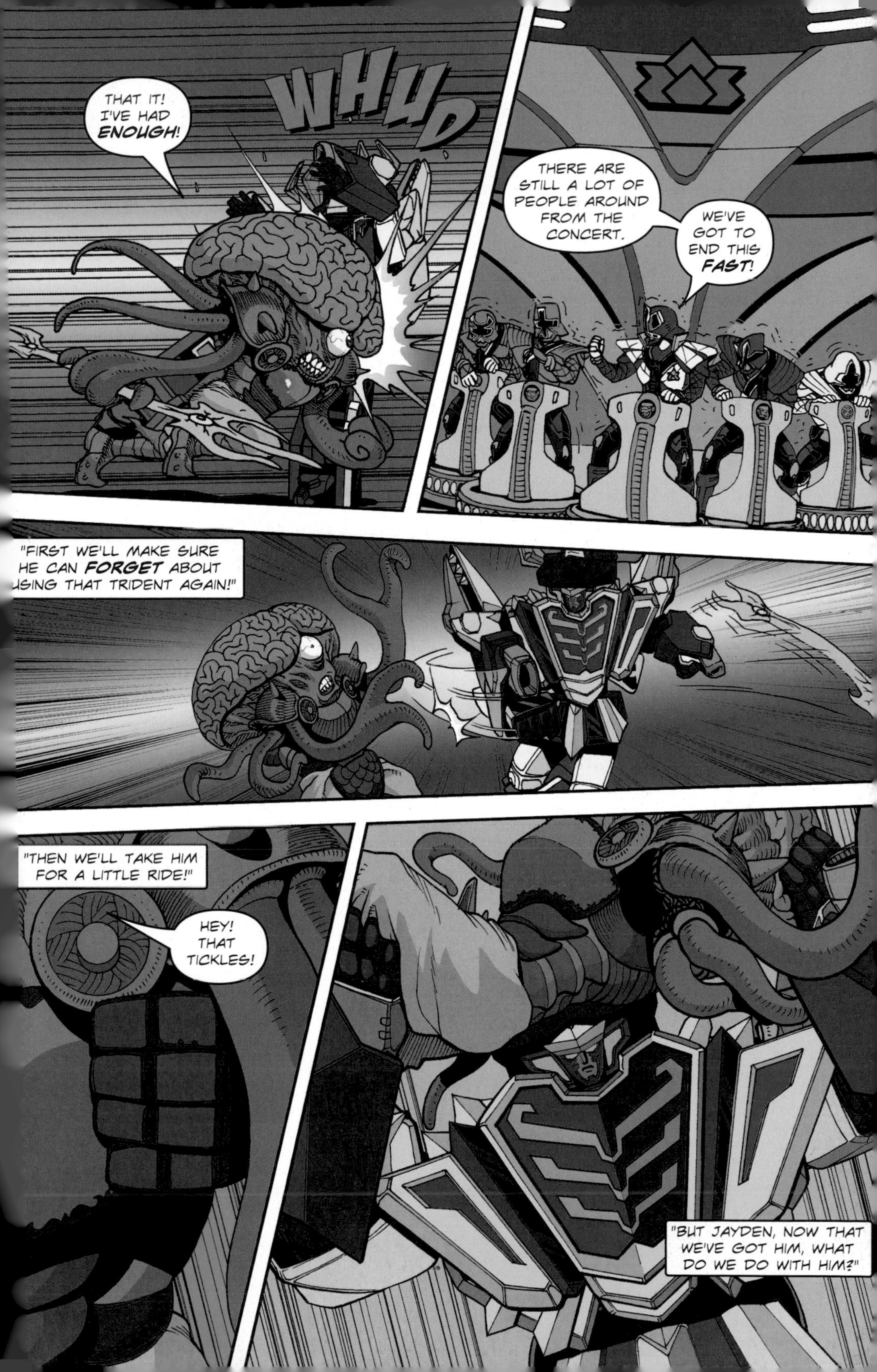
THAT IT! I'VE HAD ENOUGH!
WHUD
THERE ARE STILL A LOT OF PEOPLE AROUND FROM THE CONCERT.
WE'VE GOT TO END THIS FAST!
"FIRST WE'LL MAKE SURE HE CAN FORGET ABOUT USING THAT TRIDENT AGAIN!"
"THEN WE'LL TAKE HIM FOR A LITTLE RIDE!"
HEY! THAT TICKLES!
"BUT JAYDEN, NOW THAT WE'VE GOT HIM, WHAT DO WE DO WITH HIM?"

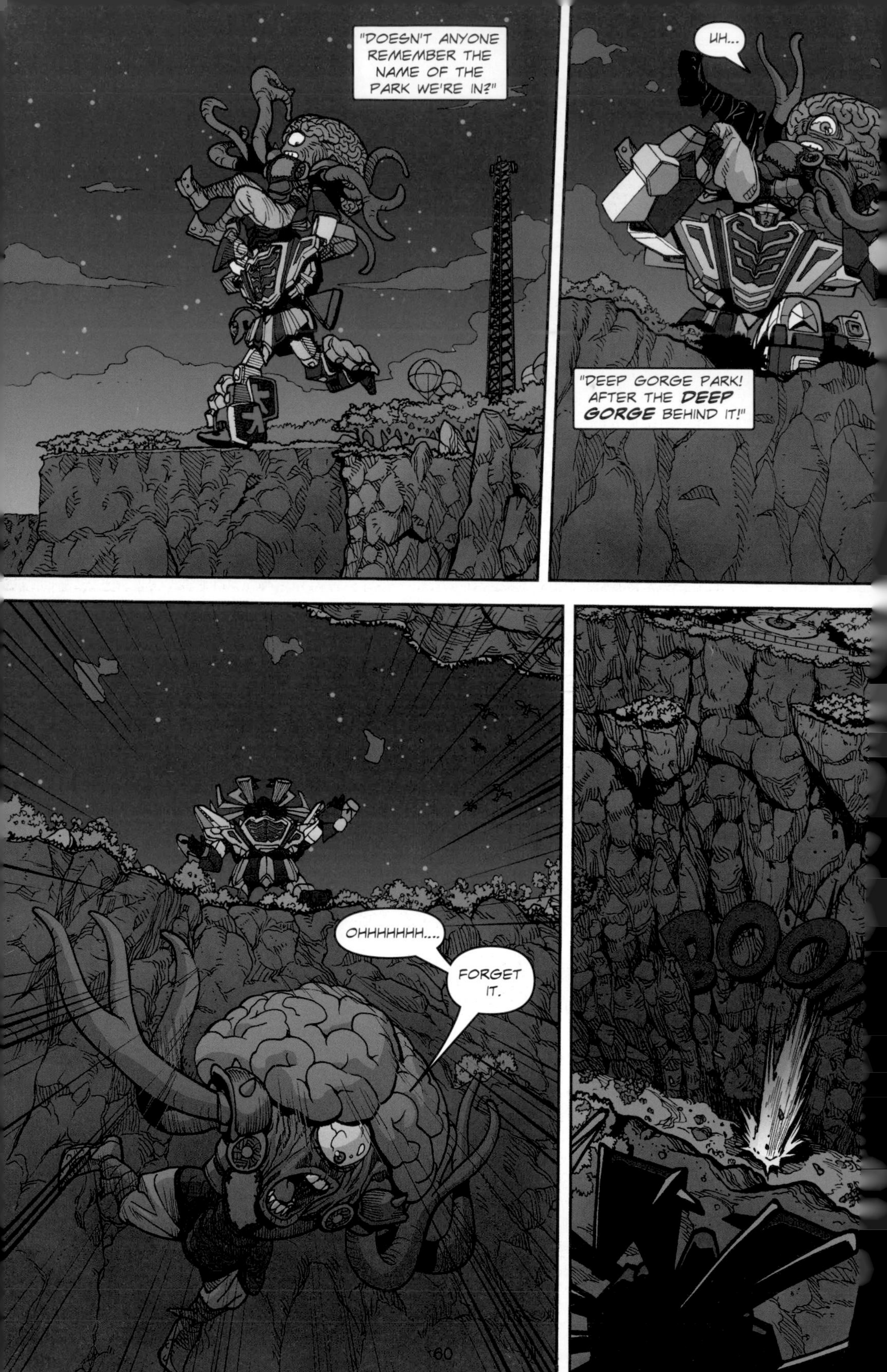
"DOESN'T ANYONE REMEMBER THE NAME OF THE PARK WE'RE IN?"
UH...
"DEEP GORGE PARK! AFTER THE ***DEEP GORGE*** BEHIND IT!"
OHHHHHHH....
FORGET IT.
BOO

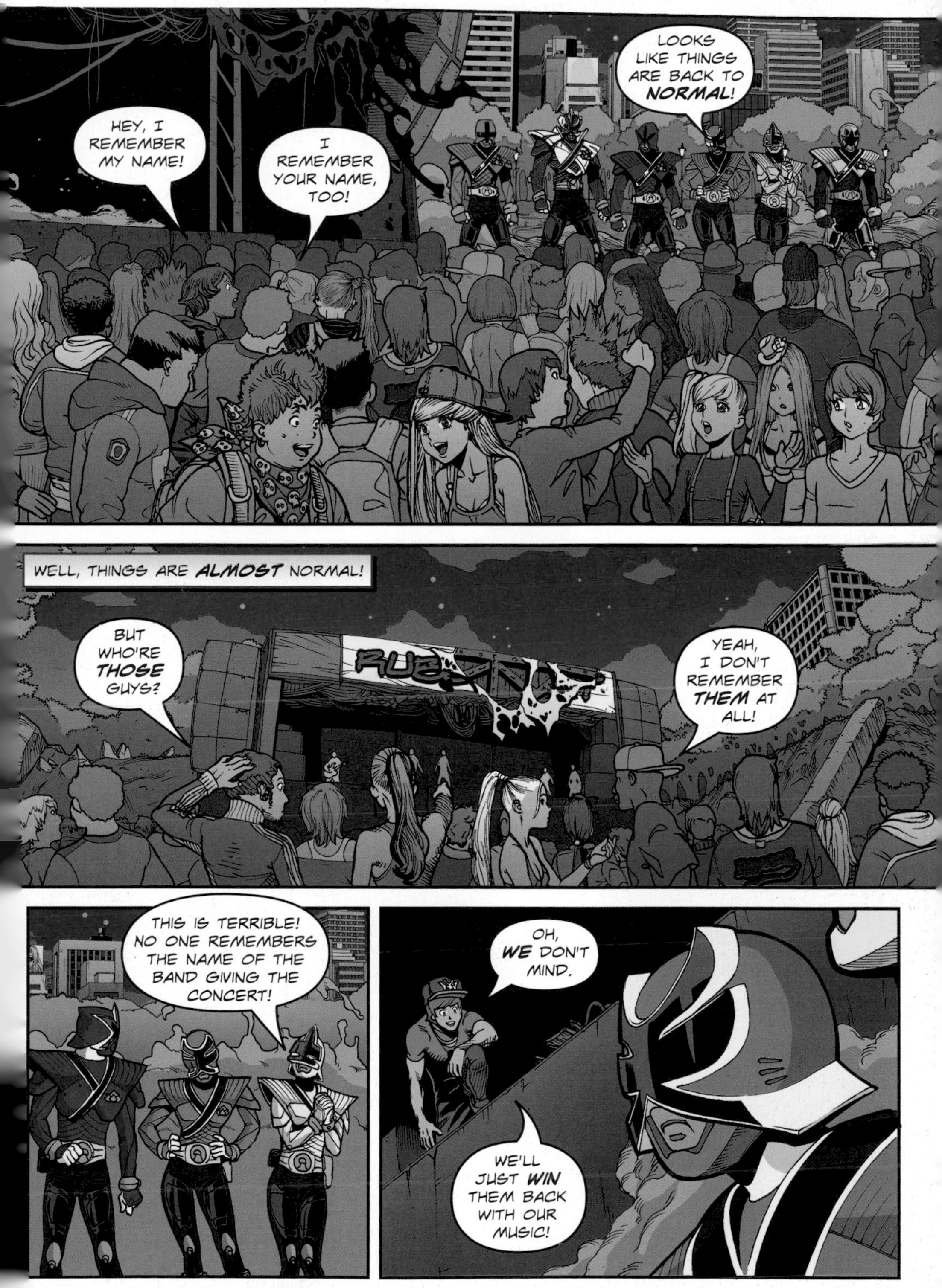
HEY, I REMEMBER MY NAME!
I REMEMBER YOUR NAME, TOO!
LOOKS LIKE THINGS ARE BACK TO NORMAL!
WELL, THINGS ARE ALMOST NORMAL!
BUT WHO'RE THOSE GUYS?
YEAH, I DON'T REMEMBER THEM AT ALL!
THIS IS TERRIBLE! NO ONE REMEMBERS THE NAME OF THE BAND GIVING THE CONCERT!
OH, WE DON'T MIND.
WE'LL JUST WIN THEM BACK WITH OUR MUSIC!

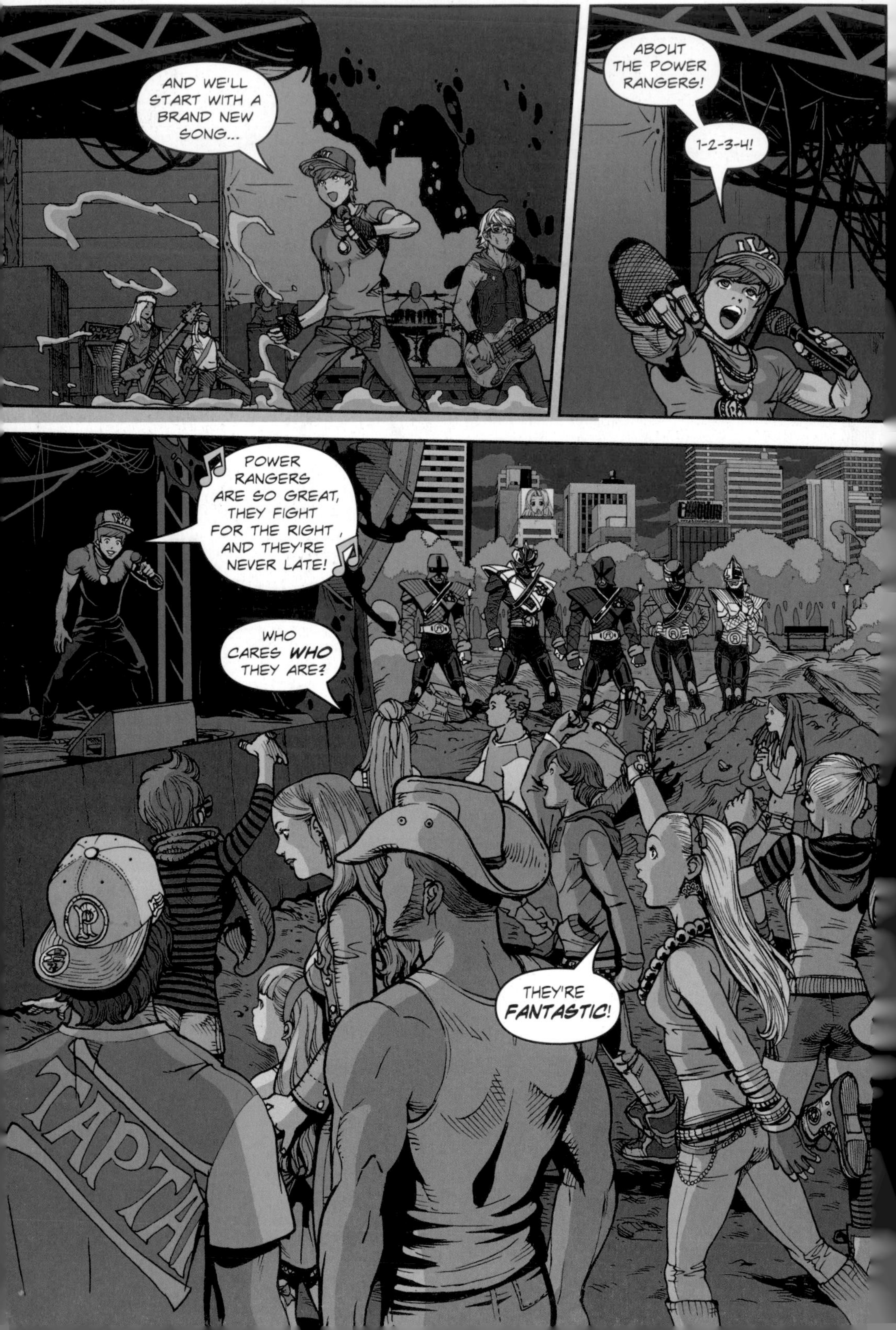
AND WE'LL START WITH A BRAND NEW SONG...
ABOUT THE POWER RANGERS!
1-2-3-4!
POWER RANGERS ARE SO GREAT, THEY FIGHT FOR THE RIGHT , AND THEY'RE NEVER LATE!
WHO CARES WHO THEY ARE?
THEY'RE FANTASTIC!
TAPTA

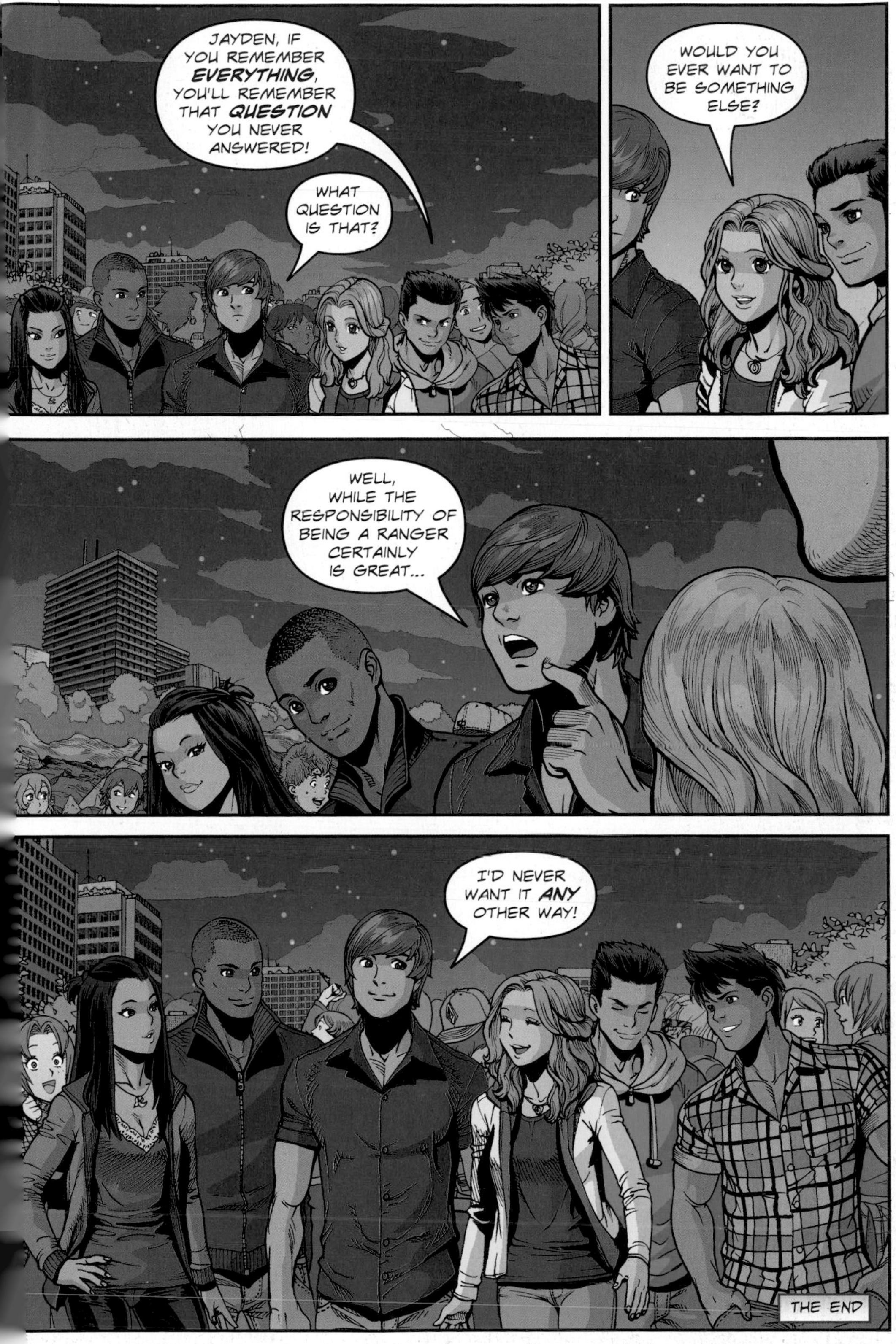
JAYDEN, IF YOU REMEMBER EVERYTHING, YOU'LL REMEMBER THAT QUESTION YOU NEVER ANSWERED!
WHAT QUESTION IS THAT?
WOULD YOU EVER WANT TO BE SOMETHING ELSE?
WELL, WHILE THE RESPONSIBILITY OF BEING A RANGER CERTAINLY IS GREAT...
I'D NEVER WANT IT ANY OTHER WAY!
THE END

WATCH OUT FOR PAPERCUTZ

Welcome to the pulse-pounding premiere of the SABAN'S POWER RANGERS SUPER SAMURAI graphic novel series from Papercutz. I'm Jim Salicrup, the Editor-in-Chief of Papercutz. Papercutz publisher Terry Nantier and I thought the time was right to bring the longest-running TV super-heroes to graphic novels, and fortunately our friends at Saban Brands agreed. To make sure this debut was worthy of the POWER RANGERS we went directly to our top-talents to find the very best writer and artist team—Stefan Petrucha and Paulo Henrique. Here's a brief biography of my ol' pal, Stefan Petrucha...

Born in the Bronx, Stefan Petrucha spent his formative years moving between the big city and the suburbs, both of which made him prefer escapism. A fan of comicbooks, science fiction and horror since learning to read, in high school and college he added a love for all sorts of literary work, eventually learning that the very best fiction always brings you back to reality, so, really, there's no way out.

An obsessive compulsion to create his own stories began at age ten and has since taken many forms, including novels, comics and video productions. At times, the need to pay the bills made him a tech writer, an educational writer, a public relations writer and an editor for trade journals, but fiction, in all its forms, has always been his passion. Every year he's made a living at that, he counts a lucky one. Fortunately, there've been many.

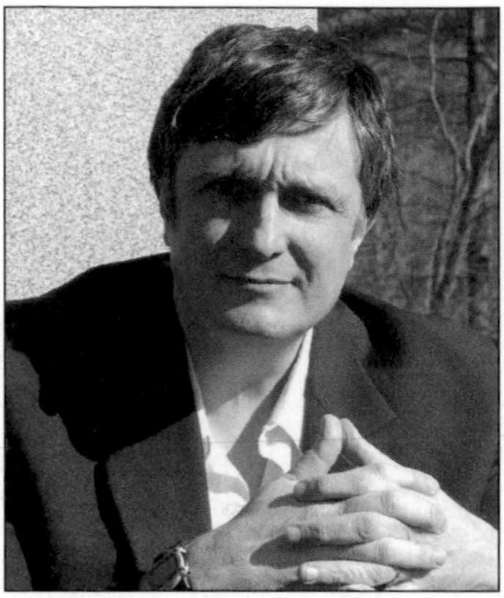

Over the years, I've been fortunate to have the very talented Mr. Petrucha write many comics that I edited; titles such as WEB OF SPIDER-MAN (at Marvel Comics), DUCKMAN, THE X-FILES (at Topps Comics), NANCY DREW, PAPERCUTZ SLICES, and THE THREE STOOGES (at Papercutz). But that's just the tip of the literary iceberg. Stefan's written many other comics, such as MICKEY MOUSE, META-4, SQUALOR, and many more, as well as such prose novels as Ripper (Pholomel), Dead Mann Walking (Ace Books), Blood Prophecy (Grand Central Publishing), Paranormal State: My Journey Into the Unknown (with Ryan Buell; Harper Collins), and many others. Despite knowing Stefan, and being familiar with his work since we were both kids back in the Bronx, he continues to surprise and delight me with every word he writes.

I'm sure there will be lots of surprises, as well as lots of exciting action, and a short biography of Paulo Henrique (who prefers to be known as "PH") in SABAN'S POWER RANGERS SUPER SAMURAI #2 "Terrible Toys" coming soon. Oh, and don't forget to tell us what you thought of this premiere Papercutz POWER RANGERS graphic novel by Papercutz! Send your comments to me at: Jim Salicrup, Papercutz, 160 Broadway, East Wing, New York, NY 10038 or email me at salicrup@papercutz.com. We know there are many loyal POWER RANGERS fans out there, and we"ll be eagerly waiting to hear your feedback.

Until then, be sure to check out www.papercutz.com for all the latest news and information on the POWER RANGERS graphic novels, as well as the many other great graphic novels created for all-ages published by Papercutz. And remember, if Master Xandred, Octoroo, or Dayu happen to invite you to a party of any kind, simply say "no," and contact the POWER RANGERS immediately!

Thanks,

Jim